A Christmas to Remember

A Christmas to Remember

PENNY ZELLER

Dedicated to all of those who seek to be Jesus' hands and feet.

For unto us a child is born, unto us a son is given: and the government shall be upon his shoulder: and his name shall be called Wonderful, Counsellor, The mighty God, The everlasting Father, The Prince of Peace.
Isaiah 9:6

CHAPTER ONE
HILLTOP, MONTANA, 1906

SOMETIMES GOD'S TUG ON a man's heart was mighty strong.

Such was the case at church on a blustery Sunday in December.

Otis, Ma, Mart, and Grandma were the only ones in Otis's family able to attend church on this particular Sunday. As a matter of fact, the congregation consisted of ten people. There was no one to play the piano, and only one elder was present. After the regular services, Pastor Gunderson rifled through a stack of papers on his pulpit.

"I do appreciate you all coming today. As you know, more townsfolk have fallen ill with influenza this week. Not only that, but we received a telegram from Hawthorne stating that they need immediate help. Their medicine stores have been depleted, and their one doctor is overrun with tending to people. But perhaps the most disturbing is that they have not been able to get any shipments of food in or out of the town due to the epidemic. The mercantile there is also closed due to the proprietors being sick." Pastor Gunderson allowed his gaze to travel over the congregants who filled only the two front-row pews. "We are in desperate need of somebody to take a shipment of medicine and food to our friends in Hawthorne."

Why did it seem as though Pastor Gunderson's gaze settled on Otis? But whether it had or whether it hadn't, there would be no hesitation if he was needed for such a critical endeavor. He glanced over at Ma, and she met his eye. Was she thinking the same thing?

Prayer was in order before he made this decision, but in his heart, Otis already knew the answer.

Pastor Gunderson prayed for healing for those in Hilltop and Hawthorne and for safe travels for whoever may undertake this important duty.

Otis could barely sit still while several folks asked a multitude of questions. He prayed again that if it was God's will, he would be the one to take the supplies to the people of Hawthorne.

He stood and unfolded himself from the pew. Ma rested a hand on his arm and gave him a slight nod of encouragement, and he strode up to the front and stood in line, waiting to speak to Pastor Gunderson. When it was his turn, Otis cleared his throat. "Sir, I would like to be the one to take the supplies to Hawthorne."

Pastor Gunderson answered with a weary nod. "I was hoping you would say that. We'd be much obliged, but I wasn't sure if your family could spare you for a couple of days."

"It's something I will need to discuss with them, but if it be the Lord's will, I would appreciate the opportunity."

He'd not only pray about the possibility of traveling to Hawthorne, but also that the Lord would give him the courage to again see the woman who'd broken his heart.

An hour later, Otis sat near the fireplace with the rest of his family, discussing Pastor Gunderson's request.

"I'm pretty much all the way recovered," said his younger brother, Mart. "I'm able to handle things around here."

"And I'm feeling much better," added Grandpa Vann, who received a stern look from Grandma Etta Mae.

"I don't want you overdoing it, Vann." Grandma rested her hand on his forehead and lifted the blanket to his chin, causing a giggle from Otis's younger sister, Anne-Marie, who, for the first time in several days, seemed to be recovering from her bout with the illness.

Pa's brow furrowed, and his attention veered to his broken leg propped up on a chair. It hadn't been easy for Pa to sit still during times of necessary ranch work. And even more challenging with Otis, Mart, Grandpa, and several of the ranch hands all sick due to the influenza outbreak.

"Pa, would you be amenable to me traveling to Hawthorne to take medicine and supplies?"

Otis was a grown man of twenty-three, so he hardly needed Pa's permission, but he did want his father's blessing.

"Absolutely, and I'm proud of you for suggesting it. You can take the sleigh and whatever else you need. I'm assuming Pastor Gunderson will want to collect food donations, and you'll need to stop by Doc's to retrieve medicine."

"Yes, sir. He mentioned such when we spoke at length after church."

After several more minutes of discussing the details, Otis headed for home. There was much to be accomplished if he was to leave in two days.

Otis finished his chores, then walked inside the house he'd been working on building for the past two years as time allowed. Pa, Mart, and Grandpa had assisted him when countless ranch duties didn't demand their attention.

All in all, it had come along nicely, and pride swelled in Otis's chest. While only the main floor was complete now, at some point, the home would boast an upstairs.

Fitting for the family he hoped to someday have.

There was still a lot to be done, but it had come a long way since the days of being just a dream. He stood at the front window and surveyed the vast expansion of mountains. He'd chosen to place the house in just this exact location so he could admire God's handiwork all through the year—from the green-pine hills in the summer to the colorful foliage in autumn, to the snowcapped mountains in winter—he could never tire of the magnificent scenery. To the west, he could see Ma and Pa's house, and to the east, the tree-lined road that led to Hilltop.

When Pa offered him his own piece of ranch heaven, Otis had started clearing the land that evening. A corral, chicken coop, and multiple cattle were added to what he'd accumulated so far.

God was good and the Giver of much.

Otis never wanted to live anywhere but on the ranch. Sure, he and Pa had gone on several cattle-buying and selling trips, and he'd seen various parts of the midwestern and western United States, but his heart remained in Hilltop and always would.

The only downside of having his own ranch? Some of the women in Hilltop had set their caps for him. Women whom he had no interest in beyond friendship. Women who, while nice and some even comely, weren't the ones he intended to marry.

His heart might belong in Hilltop, but it also belonged to Belinda.

He dismissed the thought that he sounded like a romantic fool. Perhaps he was. A fool for certain for having let her get away. When he arrived in Hawthorne, would she take kindly to seeing him? Would he even see her at all? Perhaps he could leave the crates of items with her pa. After all, Otis would be busy as ever if he wanted to complete the task and return home in a few days.

The last time he'd seen Belinda before she had moved to Hawthorne with her parents lingered in his mind as it often did. Things he could have done differently. Words he ought not to have said.

Like proposing to her.

But he'd never thought she'd say no.

They had failed to resolve the discord between them, even all these months later.

Otis felt a thumping against his leg, and he turned around to see his dog, Cow. He reached down, scooped up the dog in his arms, and was rewarded by doggy kisses on his cheeks and chin.

"I know what you're thinking, Cow, but no, you can't go with me. You'll be staying with Ma and Pa while I'm away."

As if the dog understood human language, she ducked her head and withheld further doggy kisses.

Otis patted her on the head. "I'll be back before you know it. Besides, you know Ma, Pa, Mart, Anne-Marie, and Grandma spoil you rotten. Not to mention Grandpa feeding you those scraps beneath the table. You know he's the only one who gets away with doing that."

Cow must have forgiven him because she snuggled closer, and her tail started to wag again. If there was ever an animal he loved, it was Cow. When he was a little boy, he'd grown up with Cow's mother, who was his most treasured pet. So treasured that she went nearly everywhere with him, even to school—much to his teacher's disturbance. The story, made famous by his parents and grandparents, was that when he was a young'un, he'd named his dog Cow because she was black and white like a Holstein. He'd missed Cow when she'd passed, but now Otis owned one of her pups, a mixture between a collie and a few other breeds—actually more akin to a mutt. His current dog, named after her mother, had wormed her way into Otis's heart from the first day.

He sauntered over near the fireplace and set Cow on the

floor. She peered up at him, brown eyes full of expectation. "I think I might be able to conjure up a snack."

Cow yipped, then proceeded to chase her tail in a circle. Otis chuckled. "Let me light a fire, then we'll see what we can find."

An hour later, Otis prepared for his trip to Hawthorne. Yesterday, on Monday, Otis had met with Pastor Gunderson and Doc in town regarding the necessary medicine and food donations, which had been piled high in the church. Mr. Smyth from the mercantile, along with the owners of the dry goods store, hardware store, and the new department store, packed numerous donated items in crates, including food, blankets, and toys for the children. The women's Bible study ladies, including Ma and Grandma, had spent the past few days baking bread, biscuits, and other foods to be sent with the canned goods and steaks that ranchers in the area donated. Mrs. Jowett offered some of her most precious possessions from her attic. Most of the folks in Hilltop were ill or in various stages of recovering from the influenza, but little stopped them from taking the time to care for the residents of the remote town a day's drive away.

Prayers were offered, including a vigil at church Sunday night. Tomorrow morning, Mart would help Otis fill the sleigh with items. And hopefully, God willing, the weather would hold as he traveled the distance to the much smaller town.

Were it not for his brother and two of the hired hands who had already recovered, Otis would have found it more difficult to leave. But the people of Hawthorne needed his help, and with no one else, he was happy to oblige. Be Jesus' hands and feet, as Ma always said.

He grabbed his Bible, knife, rifle, shaving supplies, and a change of clothes. As he opened the drawer to the bureau, his gaze lingered on the gold-framed picture.

Belinda stared up at him, a slight curve in her lips drawing them slightly upward. Her green eyes twinkled. She was the most beautiful woman he'd ever set eyes upon. He recalled the day clearly when they'd decided to have their photos taken by the traveling photographer. They had then, upon Otis's request, exchanged their photos. At first, Otis had displayed Belinda's picture prominently, but after that day when he'd opened his heart to her and revealed his feelings only to have her not feel the same, Otis had tucked the picture away. Perhaps he had somehow hoped to remove the pain from his heart and his mind by doing so.

But he knew he'd never forget her, no matter how much time passed.

As he rifled through the drawer in search of a pair of socks, his attention fell upon a small wooden box. He withdrew it and opened the lid, revealing the ring. He removed it from the box, noting how small it was and how it would never fit on one of his short, stout fingers. Otis held it in front of his face as the light flickered through the diamond. He and Pa had traveled to western South Dakota for a cattle sale. As Otis strolled along the boardwalk in the town they'd visited, he'd looked in the window of a jewelry store.

Normally, jewelry stores held no appeal to him.

However, when he'd seen the sparkling, ornate ring with its diamond in the center and leaves surrounding it, he'd stepped inside and inquired of the jeweler. He'd been told it was a ring made from the gold of the Black Hills of South Dakota. It was unlike any piece of jewelry he'd ever seen, not that he was well-versed in women's jewelry because he wasn't. But he did know one thing—it would make the perfect engagement ring for Belinda. He had planned to give it to her when he proposed last summer.

Even he was surprised he'd waited so long to ask for her hand. After all, they'd known each other nearly their entire lives. But he wasn't about to take a wife if he didn't have a home for her. And not just any home, but a home befitting of someone like Belinda. A home with a finished upstairs and a garden spot so she could plant her beloved rose bushes. He tucked the ring back into the box, placed it in the drawer, and attempted to remove the thought of marrying Belinda from his mind.

CHAPTER TWO

EARLY THE NEXT MORNING, just as the sun was beginning its ascent up the eastern horizon, Otis climbed on his horse and started toward his parents' home. There, he'd retrieve Mart, and together they would load Pa's sleigh.

Cow positioned herself right in front of him on the back of the horse. She stared up at him, her eyes barely blinking the entire time on the way to Ma and Pa's house. "I won't be gone for long, Cow. Before you know it, I'll be back and we'll be tending to chores again."

His dog released a tiny whine in response.

"If I took you with me, you wouldn't be able to spend time with Boots, and you know you would really miss him." Boots was Cow's younger brother. The two dogs were inseparable, although Cow was far more vivacious and Boots was more reserved. They were the only two pups Ma and Pa had kept from the original Cow's multiple litters.

Cow maintained her doleful stare. And when he climbed down from the horse, she resisted walking through the snow and instead nestled against him. If there were a more spoiled dog in Hilltop, Otis would be surprised.

He could smell the aroma of sausage and pancakes even before he stepped onto the porch. His stomach rumbled in response as he thought about the delicious breakfasts Mrs. Stroud cooked for the family. Juggling Cow in one arm, Otis turned the doorknob and entered the warm foyer of his parents' home.

"You're just in time for breakfast," said Grandma as she and Ma positioned plates and cups on the table.

That had been his intent because eating at his parents' home was far preferable to a few pieces of buttered bread and whatever he could scrounge up from the ice box and cupboards.

Cow squirmed, and Otis set her on the floor. Boots came to greet her, and they offered their obligatory sniffs before plodding toward the fireplace and settling in front of its warmth.

Pa, his leg propped up, sat at his place at the head of the table and led grace before they ate. Normally, Otis would take his time chewing the delicious meal, but not today. He and Mart needed to get to the church and load the sleigh so he could be on his way. No sense in dallying.

Otis looked around the table at his family. His grandparents, Etta Mae and Vann Davis, were actually his great-grandparents, but he'd always referred to them as Grandma and Grandpa. Grandpa was mentioning how he couldn't wait to eat cake again, and Grandma was telling him he'd do nothing of the sort since there would be nothing but healthy foods for him for the time being. Pa was talking about how he read in the newspaper about the

Petrified Forest in Arizona and how it was now a national monument.

Otis shoveled another bite of pancake into his mouth. He glanced outside and saw a few stray flakes falling from the sky. He'd need to leave soon.

"Too bad the weather isn't nicer and the roads aren't cleared," said Mart.

"I've never known a time when the roads were clear in Hilltop in December," said Grandpa, who then launched into a story about the winter of '83.

"If we didn't have such harsh winter weather, Otis could take Pa's touring car."

That caught Pa's attention. His gaze flickered between Mart and Otis.

"If it were nice weather and the roads were clear, would you allow me to drive your touring car?" Otis knew Pa's automobile was among his favorite possessions. He'd purchased it earlier this year and had it delivered all the way from Michigan. It had cost him $2,250, but his investment came complete with a horn and lamps. Otis had driven it once.

Ma's eyes twinkled. "I'm sure Pa would allow you to drive his touring car for such an important mission."

Pa wrapped his arm around Ma and planted a kiss on her cheek. "Perhaps."

His father was one of the most generous people he knew, and Otis surmised that Pa would readily share the automobile if it meant getting the food and medicine to those in need much quicker.

"Alas," Pa said. "You'll have to take the sleigh. With the

automobile's thin wheels, you would never make it through the snow drifts, although they did conduct some tests on bad roads and the touring car performed well."

Grandpa stroked his gray-bearded chin. "And reckon I heard about the Oldsmobile climbing Mount Snowdon in Great Britain."

Anne-Marie swirled some syrup on her pancakes, her face still pale from being so ill. "If it can climb a mountain, can't it traverse through snow drifts to Hawthorne?"

Grandpa smirked. "What is the horsepower on the touring car? Forty? Fifty?"

That was another thing Otis appreciated about his family—their loyalty, and in this case, their banding together in an attempt to convince Pa.

"I think we'll stick with Otis taking the sleigh." Pa attempted to sound firm in his words, but the glint in his eye told of his amusement.

After they had finished eating, Anne-Marie raced upstairs to her room and returned with her hands behind her back. "As promised, I have something for you and Cow. First, for Cow. Close your eyes and open your hands."

Otis did as directed. Anne-Marie placed two items that felt like knitted material into his hands. He opened his eyes to see a green-and-beige hat and what appeared to be a pink, blue, and gray sweater for Cow. Anne-Marie looked at him expectantly. "Thank you."

"You are most welcome. I'm sorry there's a larger hole on the very top where the yarn separated a bit, but I don't think it will show, because of how tall you are. I'm adept at sewing, but I need more practice at crocheting."

"It looks mighty fine to me, and I appreciate it, Anne-Marie. I know it's bound to get cold on the trip." He stretched the knitted hat over his round head.

Anne-Marie chewed on her bottom lip. "Is it too small?"

While the hat failed to completely cover Otis's ears, he would do nothing to discourage his sister's enthusiasm. "I think it fits great."

Anne-Marie beamed. "Now try on Cow's sweater. I didn't want her to be cold while you two are on your journey."

"I'll try it on Cow, but she won't be accompanying me."

At the sound of her name, Cow's head jerked up, and she barked.

"Why can't she go? You know she'll miss you something fierce."

"It's a long way, and she'd be better off staying here."

Cow rose from her warm spot in front of the fireplace and toddled over. She raised a paw onto Otis's leg.

"Poor Cow. Look at her sad eyes. She'll be ever so despondent if you don't allow her to accompany you."

As if on cue, Cow hung her head slightly, then peered back up at him with what did, indeed, appear to be sad eyes.

"You sound as though you are her advocate."

Anne-Marie bobbed her head. "I am. You really need to take her with you."

Otis figured if Anne-Marie didn't have Boots, she'd insist Cow stay behind. He reached down and attempted to put the sweater on Cow. She wiggled and hopped about on three legs as Otis struggled to secure the clothing. When he finally finished, he noticed that just as with his hat, there were some gaping spaces in the yarn.

Anne-Marie clapped her hands and beamed. "Perhaps I could sell some of these at our store in town."

"Spoken like a true entrepreneur."

His sister's smile covered her entire face. "Yes, I just might do that—after I improve my crocheting skills, that is. Perhaps I could knit a shirt for you next, Otis."

Otis wasn't sure he'd appreciate a crocheted shirt, but if it assisted Anne-Marie in her dream to sell knitted items in the store, he'd gladly wear it.

After several minutes of Anne-Marie declaring the positive aspects of allowing Cow to travel with him, Otis finally relented.

"Oh, one more thing before you go." Ma gestured for him to follow her into her sewing room.

Years ago, Pa had completely remodeled the former downstairs bedroom and turned it into a sewing room for Ma. Now she had the finest and newest sewing machine, bolts of fabric, and a drawer full of needles and thread. On the table nearby was a sketch pad where Ma sketched her latest fashions. She had a stellar reputation in Hilltop and the surrounding towns for her beautiful creations.

Ma handed him something wrapped in brown paper. "This is the skirt I made for Belinda. Would you mind delivering it to her?"

"I'm not sure I'll be seeing Belinda." He took the package and held it in his hand. Would he see her? Would she want to see him?

Ma reached up and squeezed his arm. "I do hope you and Belinda will work out your differences. You were once so close."

Otis swallowed the lump in his throat. They *had* been close. Belinda Finnegan's beautiful face flashed in his mind, even as regrets persisted. "All right, Ma, I'll deliver this to her. Or if I don't see her, I'll have one of the other townsfolk take it to her."

Ma smiled. "Thank you, sweet boy."

She had called him her sweet boy ever since he could remember, even though he'd been somewhat ornery a time or two in his younger years. But he would miss her term of endearment if she didn't say it.

"Your pa and I are so proud of the man you've become." Otis allowed the words to seep deep into his heart. "Have safe travels, and we'll see you when you return." She handed him a small bag of chocolates from the mercantile —his favorite. "For when you need something along the way."

Otis bid his family farewell, motioned for Cow to join him, then he and Mart hitched up the horse and left for town.

Two hours later, the sleigh loaded and Cow barking in anticipation of leaving, Otis bid Mart farewell.

"Don't worry about our family. I'll take good care of them while you're away."

Otis put a hand on his younger brother's shoulder. "I know you will, and I appreciate that."

Mart beamed. "Might be my opportunity to show Pa I'm ready to take on more responsibility."

If Mart had his way, he'd *run* the ranch. The young man had ambition in droves. "I don't think Pa has any doubt in your abilities."

"No, I reckon not, but I still want to prove to him that I'll be ready for my own place soon."

His brother had always been determined and desirous of keeping up with Otis, especially when they were young'uns. Otis doubted Mart ever figured himself "too little" or "too young" to do anything he set his mind to. "Won't be long until that day comes."

"I might be lacking in patience for that time to arrive." Mart's wide smile covered his face.

Otis playfully slugged his brother in the arm. "I tend to agree with you on your lack of patience."

"It's just that…" Mart blew out a deep breath. "I've been thinking about my future and all and asking Euphemia for her hand in courtship. A woman like Euphemia isn't liable to marry a man who doesn't have his own cabin."

It was no surprise, given how Mart felt about the young woman who'd moved with her family to Hilltop two years ago. "Mighty wise of a man to think of his future, but he ought not to let that get in the way of him living in the present."

"Now you're sounding like Pa."

Otis laughed. "It's my job now that I'm a mature man in my early twenties to start sounding like our father."

Mart tilted his head to one side. "What do you think about seeing Belinda again?"

Otis hadn't shared details of his and Belinda's discord, although he knew his family wondered. It was also likely that Ma and Grandma had guessed some of it, and Anne-Marie, with her fanciful notions, had surmised details. All three had been particularly close to Belinda, her ma, and her two sisters. "I'm not sure I'll see her. Ma wants me to deliver a skirt to her, but I might leave it with someone else to deliver. Besides, I plan to spend most of my time distributing goods to the people in need, instead of prattling on and visiting."

Even in his own ears, his flimsy excuses sounded weak. He'd like nothing more than to *prattle on* with Belinda. To enjoy the times they once shared. To hear how she was doing and comfort her if things had gone awry. Would he stumble all over his words like a hopeless oaf?

He'd rehashed in his mind at least a dozen times what he would say to her when he did see her for the first time. Her parents' ranch was on the way into the town of Hawthorne. If it was late enough in the evening, he would stop there first.

Not that he had to, as the two miles into town wasn't much further, so he'd likely drive right past her house. And if her family fared well and wasn't struggling with lack of food and medicine, it was likely he'd not see her at all.

Why did that thought both relieve and disappoint him?

"Well, I sure hope you two work it out."

Otis's attention reverted to his brother, whom he'd forgotten was standing there awaiting his answer.

"Me too. Thank you for taking care of the family while I'm away."

"Sure."

Otis studied his brother. They were so different in

appearance and personality. Otis favored Ma with his dark hair and brown eyes. Mart resembled Pa with his lighter-colored, sandy-brown hair and blue eyes. Yet, Mart was shorter and smaller-boned, more like Ma, although he was far from being weak, with his strenuous, wiry muscles and strength enhanced by years of hard work.

He extended his hand and shook Mart's before folding him into a quick side hug. "I best be on my way as daylight is getting away from me."

"Safe travels."

Otis nodded. He climbed into the sleigh and beckoned the horse. Mart waved until Otis traveled far enough down the hill and out of sight.

Lord, please watch over my family, give me safe travels, and please help me not to be too late for those in need.

CHAPTER THREE

GOD WAS SLOWLY HEALING her family.

Belinda returned from assisting Ma with eating some broth. The going had been slow, but Ma was now able to, for the most part, feed herself. Her strength was returning, and it would be only a matter of time before Ma was able to relocate from the bed where she'd been for the past nearly two weeks.

Belinda's younger sister, Mara, was asleep after a fitful night of coughing, so Belinda opted not to awaken her but instead wait until later to urge her to eat.

She hung onto the railing, ensuring her still-weak legs would sustain her, and walked back down the stairs to the kitchen. Her older sister, Leah, was scooping broth into bowls for the rest of the family. Belinda's legs, where the influenza had settled the worst during her illness, still threatened to give way beneath her now and again. But she was grateful she felt better than she had a couple of days ago.

Belinda would take any amount of improvement, no matter how minor it may seem.

Pa sat conversing with Leah's husband, Tom, who held

their sleeping daughter, Ethel, on his lap. Belinda and Leah carried the bowls and the plate of warm bread to the table. Leah gently lifted her daughter from her husband's arms and settled her on the sofa in the adjacent room before returning to eat.

Tom led the prayer, and they began to eat. Pa's hand shook as he delivered a bite of the savory soup to his mouth. It spilled midway there, and he lifted a napkin to wipe his chin. Frustration consumed his countenance. Belinda's heart broke for the man who'd formerly been so strong and robust—nearly invincible in her mind. He had lost so much weight during his time of being ill, and his gaunt face and the dark circles beneath his eyes worried her. This influenza had taken its toll on so many, even claiming the lives of a few of the townsfolk. There had been times when Belinda wasn't sure her own family would recover.

"Are you sure you don't need anything before we leave?" Tom asked. His gait still unsteady, there was likely not much Tom could do, but Belinda appreciated his offer.

"I think we'll be all right." Pa's voice shook as he said the words. It had been a challenge for him to accept help, but when the illness rendered him incapable, he'd had to swallow his pride and allow others to assist.

Leah reached over and squeezed Belinda's hand. "I can stay if you need me to."

"No, I think we'll be fine. Pa is doing so much better—and really, Ma is too. Mara is still struggling, so I will be thankful when Doc makes his rounds tomorrow."

Pa agreed with a slow nod. As the only child of his own

parents and later a man who ran a successful ranch, Pa had always been overly capable. He wanted—needed—to feel as though he still was competent. "I am doing much better, so I'm confident we'll be fine." His tone was much quieter than it had ever been. It was as if it were a struggle for him to even speak.

Belinda tossed a covert glance at Leah, and her sister gave a slight bob of her head. How could they encourage Pa in his desire to resume ranch duties, but at the same time, respectfully preclude him from overdoing it?

"It'll be good to hear what Doc says," offered Tom. "And to hear how other folks are faring."

Belinda wasn't sure how Doc had been able to keep up with the constant demand of sick people in Hawthorne. He'd finally given every family a day that he would be back by to check on them. If someone needed him beforehand, they could fetch him in town if he was in his office or leave a note for him to read between rounds.

After breakfast, Belinda assisted Leah with packing their few belongings while Pa and Tom hitched the horse to their sleigh.

Leah folded Belinda into a hug. "I just feel so bad leaving you here to take care of everyone."

Belinda looked into her sister's eyes—eyes so much like their father's. Leah favored Pa with his blond hair and brown eyes, while Belinda favored Ma. Leah's eyes were still droopy, and Belinda knew the cough, sore throat, and weakness that had been so prevalent with this illness tarried, especially the unrelenting fatigue and the cough, which was worse at night. "Truly, we'll be fine. But are you sure you'll be all right?" The trio had stayed at their house for the duration of the worst of their illness so they could all help each other.

"Yes, I think we'll be fine."

Belinda smiled. "At least you may get a little more sleep than you have been getting."

"That's a possibility. As we've joked about several times during the past two weeks, we could start a coughing choir. Honestly, though, we would stay even longer if Tom's boss didn't want him to return to do paperwork and tend to any stray customers who may wander through the door."

Belinda agreed with her sister that the prospect of townsfolk patronizing the bank—or any of the businesses—was slim, but Tom's boss in Missoula hadn't been particularly sympathetic to the town's plight.

"Thankfully, we still have one of our hired hands who hasn't succumbed to the illness yet, so he's been doing a fine job taking care of outdoor tasks. I'll manage household duties, collect the eggs, and milk the cow. And you know Pa. He'll want to return to his chores as soon as possible."

But even as Belinda said it, she worried. Of all of them, Pa ironically seemed the most fragile.

Belinda carried her niece to the sleigh and handed her to Leah. She waved goodbye as Tom flicked the reins. Leah craned her neck and continued to wave until her family disappeared out of sight. Belinda loved that her family was close. Loved that they were there for each other and would do just about anything for each other.

And she couldn't bear the thought of losing any of

them.

It had been painful enough to have lost her brother. If he had put his differences aside, he would be here too, doing what he could to aid the family in overcoming the illness that befell them.

When Belinda returned to the house, Pa was resting on the sofa. She lifted the brown-and-yellow afghan Grandma had crocheted decades ago and placed it over him. She then set about doing chores, intermittently resting for brief intervals.

That evening after she'd coaxed Mara into eating some of the broth for supper, Belinda climbed into bed. She reached for her Bible and opened it to the page where the ribbon marked her place in God's Word. She read for the next several minutes before launching into a prayer of gratitude and a few specific requests, namely, that the Lord would completely heal her ailing family.

She returned the Bible to the small wooden dresser beside her bed and opened the top drawer. Moving aside a few items of clothing, she retrieved the buried gold-plated frame.

Otis stared up at her from the picture. On that day last year when the traveling photographer visited Hilltop, she and Otis laughingly joked about getting their photographs taken. They'd had to wait a substantial time in line, as they weren't the only ones who thought it was a worthwhile idea to forever capture a moment in time.

Most of the townsfolk posed for family photographs, including both hers and Otis's families, later in the day. Neither family had known that Belinda and Otis had arrived earlier for their single pictures.

When the photographer returned to Hilltop with the portraits, Otis suggested he take her picture and she take his. Lovely idea, really, and as best friends, it was nothing out of the ordinary to suggest such a proposition.

They ventured to the mercantile where Otis purchased two frames—the finest Mrs. Smyth carried in the newly-enlarged and expansive store. The ornate decorations on the gilt frame were far more elegant than any Belinda had ever seen.

Belinda and Otis then journeyed to their favorite picnic area by the creek. They walked a short distance to the enormous flat rock and inserted their photographs into the frames.

"Close your eyes and open your hands," Otis had said after they had finished. She did as he requested, and he placed the frame with the picture of him in it in her palm.

She asked the same of him before placing her photograph in his outstretched hands.

Then they both laughed. She could still hear his handsome and joyous chuckle. It was as though they were two young children exchanging Christmas presents.

And then he'd held her gaze for what seemed like minutes. Would he ask to court her? If so, she would surely agree. If he did, she knew Pa would be amenable to his request.

But Otis hadn't asked her that day. He'd waited until the day when she couldn't say yes.

Now Otis's dapper face stared up at her—that glint in his eyes, while not fully captured in a photograph—was there nonetheless. Most people didn't smile in photographs, but Otis had. For as long as she'd known him, he espoused a cheerful countenance—an optimist while she tended to be more of a realist. They balanced each other perfectly in so many ways, and she'd entertained more than once the possibility of someday becoming his wife.

Until he'd proposed and she'd broken his heart.

Tendrils of thick regret lodged within, threatening to choke her.

Otis hadn't asked again after she rebuffed him. The day she left with her parents, he'd graciously bid her goodbye, for Otis was rarely anything but kind. But she'd seen the pain in his eyes.

Although on that day, with so much loss, she was helpless to do anything about it.

She returned her attention to the framed photograph. A dimple shone in his left cheek, and his dark hair had been slightly ruffled that day, adding to his handsome charm. She recalled that moment as if it occurred yesterday. He'd dressed in his Sunday finest, a blue shirt that accentuated his broad shoulders. She'd worn her favorite dress, and after their appointment with the photographer, they'd gone for an early supper at Lobb's Restaurant. As was usually the case, they shared in pleasant camaraderie. She often thought he knew her better than she knew herself.

Which made it all the more painful that she had done what she did.

Had Otis kept her photograph? Was it tucked inside a drawer as well? If so, did he gaze upon it from time to time? Or had he removed her from his mind? Had he found someone else? Someone so godly, so thoughtful, so dapper and strong would surely have turned his focus to one of the many women in Hilltop seeking his attention. While Otis wasn't perfect, he was perfect for her.

If only she hadn't discarded his love.

What was he doing right now? How was his family? Had he finished the house he'd been so steadfastly building?

Did he miss her like she missed him?

If she were honest with herself, she would admit that she still loved him—would probably always love him. But she doubted there was any way for reconciliation.

In her second drawer was a pile of letters she'd written to him but had never mailed. Letters detailing her regret. Pleading with him for his forgiveness.

Petitioning him for a second chance.

She swallowed the thickness that had formed in her throat. She had been so foolish. Not that she couldn't justify her actions at the time with all that had been going on and the grief that had engulfed her and her entire family from losing three people at once, but she *had been* foolish.

Belinda planted a kiss on the frame of the photograph, then placed it back in the top drawer and snuggled beneath the quilt. She folded her hands and offered one more prayer to her Heavenly Father, for she knew He heard all prayers, big and small.

And, Lord, if at all possible, might I someday have the opportunity to apologize to Otis?

True to his promise, Doc arrived the following day. "I apologize for the lack of medicine. I've had to save what little there is left for the sickest of our townsfolk."

Belinda nodded. "I understand. How is everyone faring?"

A shadow of sadness fell on Doc's face. "We lost another yesterday."

"I'm so sorry to hear that."

"We were able to send a telegram to Hilltop and ask if there might be a way they could deliver more medicine to us. Being such a small town, having no railroad, and with our freighter being critically ill, we have no way to receive necessary supplies. We figured it was the only way." Doc hung his head in defeat. He took his role not only as a doctor but also as a town leader seriously. "We also asked if they could spare any food, and if so, if they might be able to deliver some to us as well."

"I will pray they'll respond to the telegram." There was no telling how many people were ill in Hilltop or if anyone was able to work at the telegraph office. If only Hawthorne had a telephone switchboard like Hilltop did. Such a manner of communicating was surely quicker and more reliable than the telegraph.

Was Hilltop all but shut down as well? With its more sizable population, the chances were slimmer, but the way this influenza spread so rapidly, it wasn't out of the question.

"How are you feeling?"

Doc's question interrupted her musings. "Stronger and much better every day."

Doc removed his stethoscope and listened to her heart and lungs. "Your lungs sound clear. And how is the ache in your legs?"

"Less each day."

Doc smiled for the first time since he had arrived. "Now that is the news I like to hear. And the rest of your family?"

Belinda informed him about Leah and Tom's departure. Doc scribbled a note on his folded piece of paper to add their home to his list of rounds. "Ma is getting much stronger and is now feeding herself. This morning she was able to get out of bed and take a few steps around the room."

"That is one of the biggest struggles with this sickness—the rapid loss of strength. I'm glad she was able to take a few steps. I'll check on her next, but I recommend she add more steps every day. It may take some time, as you know, before she can traverse the stairs."

Belinda knew that all too well. While there had been no other option but her and Leah to tend to the rest of the family, they'd both had to ease into walking.

"Mara's cough continues to be... "

As if on cue, Mara's barking cough rang through the house. Doc's brows knitted. "That is the common sound of most of the coughs I've been hearing. It has likely settled in her chest. I will be sure to check that as well." Doc placed his stethoscope back in his bag and asked Belinda to open her mouth so he could check her throat. "It's still red and raw. Do try not to overdo it, Belinda."

That was a difficult request because she had to take care of her family. "I will do my best." It's all she could promise.

Belinda averted her attention to the view outside the front window. She noticed Pa trudging toward the barn, his steps through the powdery snow even more deliberate than usual. "I am most worried about Pa. He's lost so much weight, continues to cough, and is still so weak. It's not like him not to recover more quickly."

"The influenza doesn't pick and choose who it wants to hit the hardest." Something indiscernible flashed in Doc's eyes, and Belinda feared that it might be that someone who was formerly strong, like Pa, had lost their life to the illness. But she wouldn't ask.

"And your hired hands? How are they doing?

"Two are still sick, but one has avoided the illness and has been able to continue assisting us. If it were not for him..." Belinda shuddered. If it were not for their hired hand, there would be no wood hauled in to be placed by the fireplace and no livestock tended to, unless she herself could manage such chores. Which was doubtful with her lingering weakness and so many other duties. Losing the farm was one thing. Freezing to death due to lack of firewood was quite another.

She lifted her gaze and looked into the eyes of the elderly doctor. She knew he was doing whatever he could to help those unable to undertake necessary duties. But there was only so much he could do. She offered a prayer that the Lord would give him strength and keep him healthy.

"I will be sure to pay special attention to your pa. He's a stubborn man, but sometimes those the Lord made the most stubborn among us emerge from such issues the strongest."

Belinda hoped Doc was correct. She loved Pa and was very close to him, but yes, he *was* stubborn. Likely the most stubborn person she knew.

"I will also be sure to stop by Leah and Tom's house. But you are confident they and their little one are doing much better?"

"Yes, they are." She thought of Leah's concern about leaving to go home. "The bank insists Tom return to work to oversee some paperwork. Those in bigger cities such as Missoula, where Tom's boss and the main bank are headquartered, don't understand the severity of the situation."

Belinda observed that Doc had not drunk any of the coffee she had poured for him. It was clear his mind was unsettled and his countenance burdened. "Thank you for taking care of the townsfolk, Doc. There's no way we could ever repay you for the countless hours you've expended."

"Nor would I ever expect it." He finally took a drink of the coffee. "Try not to worry about your family. I know that's easy for me to say, and I'm grateful my wife has recovered fully and that I have yet to catch this dreadful illness, but we have to remember this is in the Lord's hands."

"Yes, and I'm so grateful for the healing He has done thus far. Will you let me know if someone in Hilltop responded to our need for medicine and food? Once my family has fully recovered, I hope to help others as well."

"I will let you know, but seeing as how your house is on the way to town as one travels from Hilltop to Hawthorne, you might know before I do if whoever they send stops here first."

Belinda agreed that it could be a possibility. Who would Hilltop send? Pastor Gunderson? Barrett MacCallum? The mayor? The sheriff?

Otis?

The breath whooshed from her lungs at the thought. If so, what would she say to him when he arrived? Would he have forgiven her? Would she see him at all?

Doc excused himself, pushed back the chair, and rose. "I'll check on your mother and sister first, then we'll see about your pa."

Belinda rose as well. She would need to go outside and fetch Pa from the barn and warn him that his turn was next. She reached for her coat, hat, and scarf, pulled on her boots, and stepped into the cold December air. A stray snowflake or two fell from the sky, and clouds replaced the prevalent sunshine from yesterday. It was a gloomy day made more dismal by the biting wind whipping through the pines.

Christmas was nearly here. Would they have a tree this year? Would she and Mara rummage through the attic for their treasured Christmas decorations? Would Ma be baking her famous cinnamon rolls? Would they traverse by sleigh to church for the Christmas Eve service? Would Belinda and Leah meet at the mercantile to find special presents for their family members?

Likely not. But this year, the second most important thing after the celebration of Christ's birth would be her family's recovery from the influenza.

She found Pa sitting on an old wooden chair in the barn, his head in his hands. At first, her heart stumbled in her chest. Was he all right? But when he lifted his gaze to meet hers, she surmised he'd only been resting for a moment. "Doc is here."

"I noticed his sleigh out front." Pa twiddled his thumbs, and she noticed that even his hands had aged during the time since being ill. Prominent and strenuous veins, along with liver spots, dotted his calloused hands. "I've been worried about Mara's cough. Hopefully, he'll be able to give her some more medicine for that."

Belinda didn't tell Pa about the lack of medicine. He didn't need the added concern.

From where she stood, it looked as though a tear glistened in Pa's eye, but surely she was mistaken. She'd only seen her father cry twice in her entire life, and that was after each of her grandparents died within a week of each other. Surely he had come close when her brother left. She retrieved the wooden bench from the far wall near one of the stalls. With effort and silently bemoaning her weak arms, Belinda placed it next to Pa's chair and eased herself onto it.

Neither said anything for a time. She inhaled the scent of hay and heard the whistling of the wind through the cracks in the barn walls.

Finally, Pa spoke. "I've been thanking the good Lord

that your ma is doing so much better. I couldn't stand the thought of losing her." This time, Belinda was sure she saw emotion in her father's eyes. He and Ma had been married for many years. They had endured good times but also hardship, and through it all they had exemplified the type of marriage Belinda hoped to have someday with her husband.

Otis's face flashed through her mind, and she quickly shoved it aside. Her chance with him was over. She could now only hope that perhaps someone like Glen, who was nice, would someday ask to court her, even though she pondered if she could grow to love him. Her own throat thickened with emotion. "I'm so thankful too."

"But, Belinda girl..."

"Yes, Pa?

"I just don't—" Pa shook his head as if he had changed his mind about sharing his thoughts.

Belinda rested a hand on his thin arm. Even through his thick coat, she knew he'd lost significant weight. "Yes?"

"Ah, it's nothing."

She wanted to encourage her father to express the concern troubling him, but he was a private man.

So she waited patiently.

Pa sucked in a deep breath. "I just don't want to let my family down."

Her father had never been so forthcoming about his fears before. And truthfully, Belinda at one time incorrectly thought he didn't have any fears or worries. "You could never let your family down."

"I couldn't handle it if I lost our ranch because I wasn't

able to tend to matters."

Their ranch in Hilltop had meant a lot to Pa when they lived there. He'd worked hard to build it from nothing to something. When Belinda's grandparents died, they moved to Hawthorne because this ranch was larger, and Pa couldn't bear the thought of selling the home that held even more memories than their own home in Hilltop.

"We will do whatever it takes so we don't lose the ranch." But even as she said the words, Belinda wasn't so sure. They'd lost a lot of livestock already from the harsh winter, and then with the influenza...

"I wish I could be as sure of that as you are."

Belinda had always been under the assumption that Pa's faith never wavered. That he stood steadfast in the presence of any type of adversity that came his way. She'd seen time and again how he joined with Ma together in prayer, their hands intertwined in front of the fireplace, at the table, or outside in the pasture. They lifted their trepidations to the One who cared about and loved them. And never once in all of her growing-up years, nor in these most recent times—when her grandparents passed and her brother disowned their family—had she ever seen that strong faith falter.

Yet now she did. However, she thought no less of her father, but perhaps her respect for him edged up a notch, if that were possible.

"I do know," she said, her voice cracking, "that God will take care of us. He has been so faithful all these years."

Pa offered a slight smile. "You sure sound an awful lot like your ma. She would say the same thing." He paused.

"You look like her, too."

That was a compliment because Ma was one of the most beautiful women, inside and out, that Belinda knew. "Thank you, and I do believe the Lord will take care of us. But you..."

Pa waited for her to continue, but could she say what was really on her mind? She inhaled, exhaled, then inhaled again. "Pa, you have to be careful and allow your body to heal before you attempt to do too much."

He said nothing for several heartbeats, and she worried she might have upset him, which was not her intention. But finally, he spoke. "I know you're right, Belinda girl. But it's difficult as there's a lot to do."

"We will manage. If we were to lose the ranch—although I would never want that to happen—we would be all right. But if we lost you, we wouldn't be." She rested her head on Pa's shoulder. She could feel the bones beneath what had once been strong and muscled.

Pa leaned his head on hers, and she once again felt the comfort she'd always felt, even as a little girl. Having a strong and godly father who loved, protected, and cared for his family.

A husband and father like Otis would someday be.

Her heart grieved that she would not be the woman who would be the recipient of such dedicated love.

"You're right," said Pa. "And if I haven't told you recently, I am so grateful that you're my daughter."

Pa had said such things in the past, but for some reason on this cold day with so much uncertainty, his words meant all the more.

And Belinda tucked the words deep inside her heart.

CHAPTER FOUR

Belinda convinced Pa to return to the house where Doc was waiting. Pa begrudgingly did so and eased himself into the chair at the table. He didn't remove his coat as he usually did when entering the house, but only unbuttoned a few of the buttons to enable Doc to listen to his chest. Doc then checked for a fever and looked in Pa's throat. He asked Pa if his appetite had been lacking, to which Pa admitted it had been. Belinda could see from the expression on Doc's face that he was concerned about Pa's lack of progress.

"I do need you to rest for the next few days. We don't want you to get the worst of it back again."

"With all respect, Doc, I'm afraid I can't do that. I have a ranch to run." Pa attempted to stifle a cough, but was unsuccessful and instead yielded to the violent sputters that rattled his chest and caused him to wheeze.

The lines in Doc's forehead deepened. He rummaged through his bag and produced a bottle of cough syrup. From the way the light cast upon it, Belinda could see it was nearly gone. Doc measured out a spoonful and offered it to Pa.

"I don't want to take that if someone else needs it."

"No one needs it as much as you do right now." Doc started to say something else, then hesitated. He stared in the direction of the fireplace as if pondering his next words. "Are you still having chills?" he finally asked.

"The chills alternate with feeling like I'm burning up."

"And the aches?"

"Ever present."

Doc rubbed his temples. "I know you don't want to hear what I'm about to say, and I completely understand your desire to be able to continue working, but you need to rest."

Pa's broad shoulders slumped. "Is it really that bad?"

"The cough has settled into your chest, and you have a fever. I wouldn't want this to develop into pneumonia."

Belinda's stomach roiled as her chest tightened. She had heard of pneumonia and how dangerous it could be. She didn't want Pa to see her troubled expression, so she stood and poured from the pitcher a glass of water for both her father and Doc. When she pivoted toward them again and set the glasses on the table, she caught a glimpse of the hollows beneath Pa's cheeks. Was it possible for those hollows to be more pronounced even in the minutes between their time in the barn and now?

Pa released an extended sigh. "Is there anything else I can do besides that?"

"There are some medicinal remedies for this type of situation, and I'm hoping we will receive more soon. When we do, I will bring more cough medicine, Dover's Powder, and an opiate for the aches."

Pa's head dropped. Was it due to defeat or because he

lacked the strength to hold it up? Or both? "I'd be much obliged for that. Have you checked on my wife and Mara?"

"I did. Your wife is doing much better. Mara still has the cough and not much energy, but she's better than the last time I stopped by."

"And Belinda?"

"She's doing much better as well, but as I told her before she went to the barn, she needs to be sure not to overdo it. This is a relentless illness, and the worst thing we can do is not give ourselves enough time to heal before returning to our daily activities."

Doc's voice had taken on a stricter edge, and Belinda wondered if that's how he had to speak to his own children a time or two when they were young.

The physician retrieved some items from his bag and set them on the table. "In the meantime, I prescribe plenty of broth and lots of rest, and here is some garlic. I assume you have some cinnamon on hand? Both the garlic and the cinnamon will help with your cough."

Cinnamon was something they had plenty of, as they were anticipating Christmas with cinnamon rolls. She lifted the tin of garlic. Could Doc afford to leave such a precious commodity with them? She looked up, and he gave a slight nod.

How difficult it must be for him to attempt to determine who needed the few remaining items that would assist with healing.

Ten minutes later, with the reluctant promise from Pa that he would go upstairs and rest, Doc was on his way. He assured Belinda he would stop by again as soon as he could.

Belinda stood first and offered her arm to Pa. To her surprise, he leaned on her. His sluggish gait made it tedious for him to climb the stairs, and he almost collapsed against her once they reached the top. Belinda wondered if he ought to sleep on the sofa tonight. Just as she was about to suggest it, Pa painstakingly put one foot in front of the other and shuffled to the bedroom he shared with Ma.

The tears smarted Belinda's eyes. Should it take this long for a strong and healthy man to recover? Doc's words flitted through her mind. *"The influenza doesn't pick and choose who it wants to hit the hardest."*

Belinda returned downstairs, sat on the sofa, and clasped her hands. *Lord, I beseech Thee to heal my family. Please don't allow Pa to grow any worse in his illness. And, please, Father, give me wisdom to treat Ma, Pa, and Mara in the absence of medicine.*

The first portion of the trip to Hawthorne occurred without incident. Otis steered the sleigh carefully along the winding road, ever mindful of the strapped items in the back seat. About an hour into his journey, he pulled to the side against some trees and reached into the bag Ma had packed for him. He withdrew one of the flavorful chocolates and popped it in his mouth, savoring the taste. He then retrieved a treat for Cow. She gobbled it and lifted her paws as if to beg for more. "That's all for now. Believe me, I'd like to eat the whole tin of chocolates, but we still have a ways to go." Otis sat for a few minutes, petting Cow as he relished the pleasant winter day. An enormous flock of birds zipped through the sky above, heading in the opposite direction. While most birds migrated south this time of year, there were a few hearty varieties that remained during the cold and lengthy Montana winters.

His surroundings were surprisingly peaceful and quiet. What was the saying about the calm before the storm?

He hoped there would be no storm until he reached Hawthorne, although all signs indicated one might be forthcoming. Not that he fretted. He was as prepared as he could be. He'd packed several blankets, warm clothing, plenty of food, including sandwiches for the noonday meal, water, and his rifle, should he be stranded and need to find food when he depleted his supply.

An elk dodged to cross the path in front of him, its antlers impressive. The wind rustled through the trees, and the cold bit his cheeks. He was thankful for Anne-Marie's hat, even with the gaps. Cow perched on his lap, and he covered them both with the quilt before beckoning the horse to continue.

Traveling along at a pace slower than he would like, due to his heavy load, gave him much time to pray and think. Weighing on his mind were the ill ones in both Hilltop and Hawthorne, as well as thoughts of Belinda. Had she succumbed to the illness as well?

Doubt crept in as to what he would say if he saw her again. Hawthorne was a small town with a population of about two hundred, last he knew. Was she happy there?

Did she miss Hilltop?

Did she miss him?

He missed her and the friendship they'd once shared. If only he had left it at friendship rather than attempting to proceed toward something more.

But he couldn't help it that he'd fallen in love with her.

The sky turned a whitish color, and the snow began to fall, peacefully at first, swirling around and landing contentedly on the ground, adding to the already massive amount of moisture.

Two hours later, he stopped again, ate his sandwiches, and fed Cow. The snow had increased, and he ate as efficiently as he could. When he resumed within a few minutes, the snow grew thicker. Before long, it was a complete whiteout, and Otis could barely see a few feet in front of him.

A thread of concern wove its way through him. Last year, two men traveling from Bozeman to Hilltop had been stranded in a whiteout and had frozen to death. A local sheriff from a nearby town found them a few days later.

It wasn't a common occurrence for Otis to fret, but the thought of being trapped in the cold caused some trepidation.

The frigid snowflakes slapped against his face. "Lord, would you please see me safely to Hawthorne? Please allow me to find my way, and please heal my family and keep them safe." He paused, squinting as he attempted to see the road ahead. Another request entered his mind—much more than an afterthought. "And, Lord, give me the words to speak when I see Belinda."

The thought of her once again caused a myriad of emotions.

With effort, Otis focused on guiding the horse. He hadn't traveled to Hawthorne often, but he knew the general route to the town. A vast distance of it was lined with tall lodgepole pines, their slender trunks seeming to reach to the sky. They bent and bowed against the increasing winds. Perhaps he ought to find a shelter and wait out the blizzard. He squinted, willing his focus to clear. His eyes smarted from the stinging cold, and his fingers throbbed with numbness from grasping the reins. Cow trembled in his lap. He briefly stopped the sleigh and reached behind him for the pile of quilts stacked around all of the food and goods he was hauling. He put another blanket beneath him, then wound yet another around himself and Cow. He could see his breath in front of him, and his chin and cheeks burned. A rabbit scuttled beside the sleigh and took shelter. The snow began to blow sideways, and Otis lifted another prayer heavenward. He needed something to take his mind off the cold to end the numerous miles that still lay ahead.

When the visibility lessened even more, the horse stopped and tossed its head. Otis prompted it to the side, where they took cover beneath a canopy of trees. The sky had darkened, and time moved on, even if Otis remained still.

He lifted one of the blankets around himself and Cow and shielded them completely from the weather. There was but one downside hunkered beneath the colorful quilt—Cow's stale dog breath. He chuckled to himself and turned his head as best as he could, given the tight quarters.

Otis had no idea the passage of time, although it felt as though an eternity had passed since he'd created the blanket shelter. He flexed his fingers open and shut from time to time, then reached into his pocket beneath several layers of clothing and, with effort, extracted his pocket watch. Cow bumbled off his lap, then hastily re-situated herself after he settled back into his seat.

The minute hand clicked in his ear. The sizable black numbers on the silver-framed timepiece indicated four o'clock.

Darkness would soon be upon him. He peeked from beneath the quilt. The wind raged. But the heavy snow seemed to have lessened slightly. "We best be on our way," he said.

Cow blinked as if to beg him to stay longer.

"I wish we could, but already it will be dark when we arrive."

He hadn't wanted to bring the dog at first, but now he was grateful he had. Being stranded in a snowstorm could get mighty lonely. He flicked the reins and guided the sleigh along the road once again.

Several minutes later, he lifted his voice and sang hymns while squinting up and barely making out the trees on the side of the road. Cow joined him and began to howl, her voice contrasting with his and competing with the fierce winds. He regretted for a moment not growing a shaggy beard to warm his face. He remembered the handkerchief he carried in his coat pocket and wound it around the lower part of his face so only his eyes showed. He tightened his scarf, wrapped the blanket more securely around Cow, and again started on his way.

At some point, he again lost track of time. The snow eased, and the blur of the sun had disappeared from the horizon. The indistinct sunset caught his attention. Darkness was imminent, but the Lord had brought him through the worst.

Belinda took the fresh bread out of the oven and inhaled the scrumptious aroma. She would wait a few minutes, then slice some and deliver it to Ma and Mara. After that, she would need to step outside and check on Pa.

He had napped, then returned to the barn for some last-minute chores, much to Belinda's apprehension. A knock at the door sounded, and she wiped her hands on her apron and turned the doorknob. A gust of wind and a smattering of snow greeted her.

"Glen?"

"Hello, Belinda."

She moved aside and gestured for him to enter the house and shut the door behind him. "Is everything all right with your family?"

Glen's parents and younger sister lived just down the road. And beyond that, Glen had built his own place, a small cabin near the creek.

He shuffled his feet. "Yes, they are healing."

"I'm so glad to hear that."

Glen fidgeted and picked at a button on his coat. "I hate to ask this. "

Belinda looked into the eyes of her kind neighbor. "What is it?"

He swallowed, his prominent Adam's apple bobbing as he did so. "Do you happen to have a few food items you could spare?"

Belinda knew that Glen, as well as many of the other families in Hawthorne, had come upon hard times last year due to the drought. Many cellars grew empty. That, compounded by Hawthorne's inability to receive any shipments of food, caused a serious dilemma for many. "Yes, I would be happy to pack you a crate. I just took some bread out of the oven. Might your family enjoy a loaf?"

Glen smiled, his freckled face brightening as he did so. "We would never turn down a loaf of bread."

Belinda waved toward the fireplace. "Why don't you take off your coat and settle in by the fire for a few minutes while I gather some things?"

Without complaint, Glen did as she suggested. Belinda marched upstairs to retrieve one of the extra crates from the attic. She would need to gather more canned food, jams, and potatoes from the cellar. But for now, she had a sufficient amount for both her family and Glen's.

When she returned downstairs, she wrapped one of the loaves of bread and placed it in the crate. "Do you need some meat also?"

Glen hesitated a moment. "I have been able to shoot a rabbit or two this past week."

Which Belinda interpreted to mean that yes, they also needed some meat. "I'll add a few steaks from the ice box just in case you tire of rabbit stew." She smiled, hoping to ease some of his embarrassment. Glen's family struggled more than some in Hawthorne, but they were always among the first to help others in need.

"Thank you, Belinda. I can't tell you how much I appreciate this. You know I wouldn't ask if it wasn't absolutely necessary."

"I am just happy we can help. Did you hear that Doc has sent a telegram to Hilltop asking if someone could deliver some food and medicine to us?"

"I had not heard that." Sadness clouded his features. "I'm thankful we haven't lost anyone else to this horrific illness."

A few awkward seconds ticked by before her neighbor spoke again. He stood from his perch near the fireplace and faced her. "When this is all over, would you consider courting me?"

His question caught her unawares, and she stared at the man standing in front of her. The horizontal lines on his prominent forehead creased. While Glen was only two or three years older than she was, he had aged significantly since the illness.

Perspiration shone on his brow, and she knew he expected an immediate answer. Glen was a godly man, and would care for her and be a suitable husband and a doting father to their children.

Otis's face entered her thoughts, and with effort, she shoved it aside. Were she to wait until she patched things up with Otis, she would be a spinster for certain. Even then, who knew whether he had already married or planned to marry someone else? If, for some reason, the courtship did not go as planned, there was no obligation to marry Glen. Not that she imagined that would happen.

"If you could learn to love me in time."

Glen's words brought her back to the conversation. She hadn't known him for too terribly long, but she *could* learn to love him, couldn't she? "Yes, I will consider courting you."

Her words eased the burden on his shoulders, and he stood straighter. "Hopefully, someone from Hilltop will arrive soon."

She was grateful he had changed the topic from the awkward question of courtship. "I'm praying steadfastly for that. And for those who are ailing." She thought of Pa. She needed to go outside and ensure he was all right. Remind him of what Doc had said, and ask if she might handle the remaining chores he and the hired hand hadn't yet done, so Pa could partake in the rest his body so desperately needed. She involuntarily shivered and was once again appreciative that their hired hand had stacked more wood for them early this morning.

"Well, I best be on my way. Thank you for your generosity."

"Anytime. Please let us know if you need more. It is never any problem at all, and we have plenty." Belinda handed him the crate and then opened the door for him.

As she watched Glen climb into his sleigh, she thought about what she had promised. Yes, she would consider courting Glen, and after much prayer, she knew she could learn to love him the way a wife ought to love her husband.

CHAPTER FIVE

THAT EVENING, BELINDA STOKED the fire and watched the dancing flames as the heat radiated off them. She returned the stoker to its location just as a raspy cough from upstairs filled the air. She prayed again that God would heal her family of this terrible influenza that had struck them.

She poured some water from the pitcher, placed the three glasses on a tray along with some slices of buttered bread, compact squares of meatloaf, mashed potatoes, and bowls of applesauce, and moseyed upstairs. At the top, she paused and caught her breath. The fatigue and exhaustion were unrelenting. Shouldn't climbing a mere set of stairs be much easier by now?

When she entered her and her sister's room, Mara sat up in bed, her eyes droopy, her nose red, and chills racking her body. Belinda set the tray on the dresser beside the bed and felt her sister's forehead. It came as no surprise that she was burning with fever.

Belinda aided Mara with tipping the glass of water so she could take a meager sip. "Mara, you have to drink more than that."

Mara, who shared Pa's stubborn streak, shook her head and shivered before plopping back onto her pillow. Hopefully, it had just been Belinda's imagination that her younger sister had taken a turn for the worse.

Dehydration was a very real concern, and Doc had discussed with Belinda more than once the importance of drinking plenty of fluids. Belinda left the tray on the dresser and returned downstairs for a wet rag. It took longer than she'd hoped to return to her and Mara's room, and she'd nearly stumbled on the top stair. She collected herself and re-entered the bedroom. Belinda teetered slightly, her own exhaustion wearying her, and she gripped the side of the dresser for a brief moment and closed her eyes. Perhaps she should have agreed with Leah's suggestion to stay.

Belinda opened her eyes and gently pressed the rag to her sister's forehead. Mara reached a trembling hand toward it and attempted to shove it aside. Her teeth chattered. "I'm cold. Can I-can I have the blankets?" Her pleading tugged at Belinda's heart.

"Just one for now." Belinda folded back the other two quilts and covered Mara with the remaining one. Her sister rolled into a ball and continued to shiver. Fevers were challenging. Nobody wanted to be cold, but if Mara's temperature continued to rise...

"Are you sure you don't want some applesauce, potatoes, meatloaf, or even a slice of bread?"

The shaking of Mara's head was so slight that Belinda wasn't sure if she had imagined it. Her sister closed her eyes, and soon the shaking lessened and her soft snores filled the room.

Belinda sat on the edge of the bed for a few minutes before carrying the tray to Ma and Pa's bedroom.

Ma sat up in bed and, with Belinda's assistance, eagerly ate and drank from the portions Belinda provided. Pa's thunderous snores, in sharp contrast to Mara's, indicated he was sound asleep. She'd not disturb him.

"Belinda, thank you for taking care of us." She could barely hear Mom's hoarse voice over Pa's breathing.

"You're welcome."

Ma set a hand on Belinda's arm. "How are you holding up?"

She could see the worry etched in Ma's face. She needn't fear that Belinda couldn't care for them in addition to her other concerns. "I'm doing fine. Perhaps tomorrow you might be able to take a few more steps. Doc says that would be an excellent way to gain some of your strength."

"Yes, I would agree. How is Mara?"

"She hasn't eaten much today, but I was able to get her to sip some water."

"Maybe tomorrow she will have more of an appetite. She'll get so weak if she doesn't eat anything."

Belinda, happy for conversation, chatted with Ma for a few more minutes before taking the uneaten food downstairs. After washing the dishes, she opened the cupboard to check on their provisions. Tomorrow she would go to the cellar. They still had plenty, although their rations had dwindled significantly, especially since they'd donated many items to their various friends and neighbors.

But how could they not? So many were in a worse predicament than the Finnegans, especially since the mercantile had been unable to restock any of its food, and many gardens hadn't done well this past year, from first a drought, followed by a fierce storm of torrential rains and hail.

Pa offered to go hunting, but he wasn't feeling well enough, and Belinda had dissuaded him from such an endeavor. In his fragile condition, he could wander off and become too exhausted to return through the deep snow drifts.

She walked to the window and stared into the night. Earlier today, heavy snow had arrived, followed by clear skies and brisk winds. The moisture had added several inches to the already abundant accumulation. Fatigue overwhelmed her, and she took a seat in the chair by the fireplace for a brief moment. *Just a few minutes of shut-eye before I finish tonight's chores.*

Belinda wasn't sure how long she'd been asleep before she heard a knock. Who would be arriving at this late hour?

Her heart lodged in her ribs. Surely somebody wasn't stopping by to deliver bad news about another town resident.

She willed herself to trudge to the door. She unlocked it, turned the knob, and opened it, not sure what to expect. While she may have imagined just about anybody to be standing on the porch, she hadn't anticipated Otis MacCallum. "Otis," she gasped. "Is everything all right?

"Hello, Belinda. Yes, everything is fine." Snow crystals

clung to his chin, and prominent dark circles shone beneath his eyes. He held Cow in his arms.

They stood staring at each other. The wind whipped through her thin skirt and blew wisps of hair from her face. A gust caused the house to groan, and darkness, combined with zero visibility from the torrential snow, hindered her from seeing anything past the porch. How had Otis made it here in such a precarious storm?

Belinda returned her attention to her guest and finally found her voice. "Goodness, but where are my manners? Please do come in." She gestured for him to enter the foyer and closed the door behind him. For a moment, she wondered if her eyes were deceiving her. How long had it been since she had last seen him? Their most recent conversation had not ended well, and the regret still lingered in her heart.

She took a step back and offered to take his coat. He set Cow on the floor, unbuttoned his jacket, and handed it to her, along with his hat and gloves. She motioned for him to stand by the fireplace, and he did so.

Cow, who was dressed in her own knit sweater, tilted her head to one side and batted at Belinda's skirt. "I've missed you, Cow." She knelt to pat the sweet animal's head. Cow then circled a few times before reclining on the rug in front of the fireplace.

"Is your family...are they all right?"

He turned to face her, and her heart did a little jolt. Belinda attempted to ignore the effect he still had on her and awaited his answer.

"Reckon they're doing fine, although Anne-Marie and

Grandpa are still recovering from this terrible influenza, and Pa broke his leg slipping on the ice. Ma, Grandma, and Mart have all fully recovered from the illness, as have I."

She released a sigh of relief. "I'm so glad everyone is fine. When I opened the door and saw you there..."

"It's been a challenge in a lot of ways with this malady. We've lost a couple of friends in town."

"I'm so sorry. Was it anyone I know?"

Otis listed off the names. She knew all of them, and tears threatened as she mourned the loss of life. So sudden. So tragic. So unexpected. "We've...we've lost people here as well."

"I'm sorry to hear that. Your family...how are they?"

Their families had known each other for nearly her entire life, from the moment her parents had moved to Hilltop when Belinda was five years old. "I have since recovered, as has Pa, although he is still very weak." She thought of her father's wobbly balance, glassy eyes, and his labored breathing. His sunken cheekbones and gauntness opposite his formerly round face. "Leah has recovered, and Ma has improved, but Mara is still struggling to heal."

A part of her—a large part—secretly hoped he had come to rectify things between them. But why would he choose a snowy, cold winter day during one of the worst epidemics the area had seen?

Besides, she was to blame for the tension between them. He owed her no apology or explanation.

He must have decided to visit for a different reason. "Why did you come?"

"We received a telegram from Hawthorne's doctor

indicating that people in Hawthorne needed more medicine and food if we could spare it."

Belinda exhaled a long whoosh of air. The Lord had answered their prayers. Were it old times when she and Otis were close and the very best of friends, she would have thanked him, and he would have folded her into a reassuring hug. But alas, those days were in the past. However, she could still profusely thank him for the sacrifice of leaving the warm comforts of his ranch, of leaving his family behind when they likely needed him, and traveling all this way to Hawthorne to help a small town with no railroad and most of its population ill.

"Thank you for coming. So many of us have been praying that the telegram sent to Hilltop would result in someone arriving here to help us. We've been so desperate."

"We almost didn't receive the telegram. Our postmaster has been severely ill, and were it not for Mrs. Jowett expecting a letter from a friend back East, we may never have seen the telegram until the postmaster returned."

She offered a prayer in gratitude. "I'm so thankful. For some, it's felt hopeless, especially for those who didn't have much of a harvest this fall due to the weather."

"We were much the same, but I do have a bounty of food that many of us have gathered, and Doc packed plenty of cough syrup and other remedies." Otis stuffed his hands into the pockets of his jeans. "I do need to leave soon if I'm to make it to town before the doctor retires for the evening."

The stairs creaked, and Pa shuffled, one step at a time.

"Otis, it's good to see you."

Otis's expression told Belinda he noticed Pa's weak voice and ailing countenance as well. He shook Pa's hand. "Good to see you too, sir."

"Did I hear you tell Belinda that you're heading into town with supplies?"

"Yes, sir, I wanted to catch the doctor before he retired for the evening."

"Why don't you stay here for the evening? Go unhook your sleigh, and we can make you a bed in front of the fireplace. No sense in you traveling this late at night in the cold. There will be plenty of time to do that in the morning."

Otis appeared to be debating Pa's suggestion. Seconds ticked before he finally answered. "Reckon I might just do that. Since I won't be able to deliver anything tonight anyway, it's best to get started early in the morning."

Pa placed a hand on Otis's shoulder. "I'm sure I don't need to tell you that you're a godsend."

"I'm just glad to be able to help those in need."

"Your parents must be mighty proud of you."

"Yes, sir."

Otis had always been an upstanding and compassionate man. The regret filled her anew—she'd been so daft. Otis yawned, and Belinda knew he must be exhausted from his trip. She was glad Pa suggested he stay the night and travel into town tomorrow.

Pa teetered on weak legs. "Well, I'd best get back to bed. Thank you for driving all this way, and please make yourself at home, son." He slowly ambled upstairs.

Belinda retrieved a stack of quilts and set them on the rocking chair, along with a pillow. "What time will you be leaving in the morning?"

"I'd like to get an early start, as I know people are waiting on this medicine. I assume probably around seven o'clock, right after breakfast."

A thought horrified her. For the second time that evening, she wondered where her manners were. "Did you have supper?"

"I stopped briefly and ate some sandwiches Mrs. Stroud prepared for me."

"The meal I prepared earlier is still somewhat warm. Might I fix you a plate?"

"I never turn down a tasty meal." He smiled at her with that lopsided grin that had stolen her heart. The grin that still did.

She dipped her chin, hoping he would not see the heat that flooded her face. How could one love someone the way she loved Otis and hurt him the way she had? "I'll fix you a plate then."

"I'll unhitch the horse and be back. Is there anything I can do for you in the barn before I return?"

"If you could just make sure the animals are all right and that the eggs were gathered, that would be wonderful." She lowered her voice. "Pa is not himself, and I haven't had the chance to go outside."

Otis put on his coat and buttoned it before tugging on his hat and gloves. "I'll do that and be back in a few minutes."

She pushed aside the curtain and watched as he started

toward the barn. His lantern bobbed in the dark, now mostly clear night. She would recognize those broad shoulders and self-assured stride anywhere.

CHAPTER SIX

Seeing Belinda again had caused all sorts of emotions to jumble around in his heart and mind. Her honey-colored hair and her expressive green eyes drew him in as though there had never been any time or conflict between them. She'd been his best friend before he'd fallen in love with her.

And then, just as quickly, he'd lost her.

Otis opened the barn door and pulled the sleigh inside before unhitching the horse. He inspected the area for any eggs, checked on the animals, then fetched the brown wrapped package that Ma wanted him to deliver to Belinda that he'd forgotten when he first arrived.

Exhaustion weighed on him from the lengthy and eventful trip from Hilltop to Hawthorne.

He walked back into the house to find a plate of food on the table awaiting him. His stomach growled in response. Otis handed Belinda the package. "Ma asked me to deliver this to you."

Belinda slowly unwrapped the parcel. She set the paper on the table and held up the red skirt. "Oh, it's beautiful! Will you please tell your mother thank you?"

For a moment, Otis was mesmerized all over again. Her countenance lit with joy—the type of joy he'd fallen in love with. "Yes, I will tell her.

Bowing his head, he said grace, thanking the Lord for the safe trip, the food before him, and that Belinda's family was slowly healing from the influenza, before placing the napkin in his lap and starting first on the warm buttery potatoes.

If he weren't so hungry, he would go to sleep straightaway, but he'd never turn down a delicious supper, especially freshly baked bread. "Thank you for the meal."

"You're welcome."

Things had become awkward between them, although that could be due to the late hour. He struggled for a few more words to say before bidding her good night.

She smiled that beautiful smile that caused a dimple in her cheek—that smile he'd fallen in love with. The smile from a woman who didn't feel the same.

"Good night, Otis."

"Good night, Belinda."

Their eyes met for several heartbeats before Belinda nodded and retreated up the stairs to her room.

"Well, Cow, I guess it's time for us to catch some shut-eye." He opened his arms. Usually, his pet would run toward him. Not this time.

Cow looked at Otis, then up the stairs, back to Otis, and finally up the stairs. She'd always been overly fond of Belinda. Cow slowly walked away from Otis, her nails tapping on the wooden floor as she did so. The dog peered back at him, her large brown eyes full of apology. Or at least he thought it looked like an apology. Cow then retreated up the stairs.

"You're such a traitor, Cow."

While Otis would need plentiful sleep tonight, not only because he was still healing from the influenza but also due to the busy day ahead of him, he figured sleep would be challenging to attain.

His mind would never be far from the woman who had stolen his heart.

Belinda tossed and turned that night. It didn't bode well when she was still recovering from being so ill, but her mind stayed steadfast on Otis. She'd had the opportunity to set things to right between them tonight, yet she'd allowed so many things to go unsaid.

She rolled over as quietly as she could to avoid disturbing Mara, who had finally fallen asleep after several minutes of fitful coughing. Her fifteen-year-old sister had been among the sickest with the nasty illness.

Thankfully, Leah, Tom, and Ethel had recovered fairly quickly. It was odd how it struck folks so differently.

She squeezed her eyes shut, but all she saw was the image of Otis standing on the porch. Earlier that evening, his strong, tall, muscular frame filled the doorway. It didn't surprise her that he was the one to offer to help those in her town. That was one of the things that had long drawn her to him was his sympathy for others.

Rolling over once more, Belinda tugged the covers up just beneath her chin. Likely she would see him tomorrow morning, but then he would stay somewhere in town, perhaps at the church or in the parsonage—before returning to Hilltop.

Was there still a chance for them? Should she have sent the letters she'd written?

Glen fancied her, and he would make a suitable husband, but he wasn't Otis. Would it be fair to agree to court Glen? Especially when her heart would always belong to another? Would she even have another chance with Otis?

These questions swarmed through her overactive mind at 1:30 in the morning when she ought to be sleeping. Such important matters were not resolved in the middle of the night. More prayer was needed.

She closed her eyes and folded her hands beneath the blankets. *Dear Lord, thank you for letting Otis arrive safely. Thank you for his benevolent heart and his desire to help the townsfolk of Hawthorne. Thank you for all the people in Hilltop who donated so that so many in Hawthorne wouldn't go hungry or without necessary medicine. Lord, I pray for those who have lost someone to this awful malady. Please comfort them during their time of grief. And, Lord, please allow me the opportunity to apologize to Otis.*

The following morning, Belinda awoke early and set about

preparing breakfast. Pa and Otis had already left the house to do chores, and presumably, Otis was also hitching up the horse to prepare to drive into town. She appreciated that he was offering to assist with the necessary chores on the ranch.

The click of the doorknob drew her attention from frying the eggs, and she looked up to see her sister. "Leah!"

Belinda hurried to meet her sister halfway and embraced her. Baby Ethel squirmed in Leah's arms and reached up, patting Belinda's face. "Aunt-ee?"

She smiled at her sweet niece's vernacular and planted a kiss on her plump cheek.

Leah took a step back and thumbed toward the front door. "Did I just see Otis MacCallum out there?"

"You did."

"You didn't tell me he was coming. Did you two reconcile?"

The buoyant expression on Leah's face almost made Belinda want to tell her they had. "No, he's here to deliver medicine and food to the townsfolk. "

Leah set a wiggling Ethel on the floor, where she instantly half-crawled, half-walked toward Cow. She giggled as the dog licked her face. Leah put a hand to her heart. "That is so good to hear. There are so many in need right now. Speaking of people who aren't feeling well, how are Ma, Pa, and Mara?"

"Ma and Mara are doing better, especially Ma. Mara was finally able to get some sleep last night."

"Praising the Lord with you that they are both doing better." Her sister's shoulders rounded, and she peered down at her folded hands. "It's heartbreaking to think we've already lost a couple of members of our town."

"I can't even begin to imagine. Otis said they had lost several in Hilltop as well." Belinda shared with her sister the names of those who'd lost their lives to the sickness.

Leah clapped a hand over her mouth. "Oh, no, that is awful." They discussed for a few minutes their memories of the people who had died before Leah asked, "Are you feeling better?"

"Much better. I believe I'm fully healed, but I do worry about Pa. He is still so weak."

"The fatigue and the cough seem to be lasting the longest."

Belinda returned to the stove and finished scrambling the eggs before transferring them to a plate. "Will you be staying for breakfast?"

"I do intend to, as I would never pass up your savory cooking, my dear sister."

Belinda giggled. "I'm not sure about *savory*, but no one has yet complained that it's inedible. "

It was Leah's turn to laugh. "Now, do tell me all about Otis."

"There's not much to tell." At least not regarding the information Leah was prodding her for.

"It still befogs me to no end why you turned down his proposal."

Belinda had explained a bit to Leah, who knew more than anyone else, about the situation. She placed the plates of scrambled eggs on the table and went back for a second load. Belinda was grateful when Cow rolled onto her back and writhed on the floor with playful yips, causing Ethel to mimic her. The distraction kept Leah from questioning Belinda further.

However, it was short-lived.

"I'm surprised he didn't drive into town and stay with Pastor."

"I think he would have if it hadn't been so late when he arrived in Hawthorne. I'm grateful he made it here safely."

Leah regarded her. "And did you two talk?"

Her sister was relentless.

"We did talk, but not about *that*."

"You two have got to be the most stubborn individuals I have ever met." Leah rolled her eyes for good measure.

"It has been awkward. I do suppose I won't see him after he leaves here this morning to deliver the items."

"Surely he won't be doing that alone. Won't Pastor or Doc help him? "

"Maybe somewhat during Doc's rounds and Pastor's visits. Pastor has also been assisting those who have been unable to tend to their livestock."

"True. Poor fellow. Otis shouldn't have to assume such an enormous undertaking all by himself."

Leah should have been an actress in a play.

"And just what are you insinuating, Leah?"

"You should go with him."

Belinda sliced a few slices of bread and buttered them. "Perhaps Tom could help him. I have to stay here and tend to Ma and Mara."

"Tom is up to his eyebrows in work at the bank. As far as Ma and Mara are concerned, I'd be happy to stay here so that you can help Otis deliver the food and medicine. After all, he's not familiar with where people live in Hawthorne. "

Belinda started to argue. Leah held up a finger. "Now, now, Belinda, I believe you should be the one to go with him."

In their younger years, as the eldest, Leah had always been overly bossy. It was good to know that some things hadn't changed. "Well..." If Leah wanted to be here and tend to Ma and Mara and keep an eye on Pa, there really was no reason for Belinda not to go with Otis. Other than perhaps stubborn pride.

"But what about your husband? Won't he miss you when he arrives home?"

"I'm not planning to stay for a week. Besides, Tom encouraged me to stop by and help with any needs. I know you, Belinda, you'll try to get out of this if you can. So, I say you should just go, spend some time with Otis, help the sick and hungry, and hopefully resolve your differences."

If only it were that simple.

Otis recalled the day as if it were yesterday. He'd paced the floor over and over several times that morning before heading out to chores. He'd prayed in the days leading up to this day, on that day, and right before he'd asked her.

Yet for whatever reason, it hadn't been God's will.

Belinda looked so pretty that day, her hair pulled back

at the nape of her neck and a few freckles dotting her nose. He was sure that his life would change after he asked her the question on his heart.

It was changed forever, all right, but not in the way he had wanted.

Otis had invited her on a drive for a picnic. She had agreed, but even as they shared in pleasant conversation and traversed along the road in the buggy, he could see something troubled her.

He longed to take her into his arms and promise that he would make right whatever was bothering her.

The words between them were normally plentiful, but today things were strained for whatever reason. Grandma always said if there was nothing else to talk about, discuss the weather. *"Lovely day isn't it?"*

"Yes, it is." She had smiled at him sweetly as she always did, but this time, the smile didn't reach her eyes. He allowed his gaze to linger on her for a few more seconds before reverting his attention to the road ahead.

Otis veered the buggy around the corner and to the beautiful setting beside the creek. A yellow finch twittered by and landed on the branch of an aspen tree. The air smelled of spring and the promise of new life. He assisted Belinda from the buggy, retrieved the basket, and then prayed over the meal before they ate. The box in his pocket reminded him that today was the day he'd ask the all-important question. He'd already been clumsy once and nearly tripped over some roots from a nearby tree. Of course, given his nervousness about the whole situation, he could probably trip over a pine cone.

Would she like the ring? Would she agree to his question? Would she like living at his house— their house—on the ranch? While it wasn't completely finished yet, he'd spent a considerable amount of time building it with a future with her in mind. Would she be happy as his wife? He raised his eyes to the sky and offered one more prayer before taking a deep breath.

He rubbed his sweaty hands on the front of his pants. His mouth went dry, and he gulped a swallow. *"Belinda?"*

"Yes?"

Surely she felt for him the way he felt for her.

He nearly toppled off the log he was sitting on. When he righted himself, he lowered to one knee. Suddenly remembering that it would be more difficult to retrieve the ring from his pocket in a crouched position, he stood, withdrew the box, and held it in his left hand, then bent again to a knee.

A flash of something brewed in her gaze, and he thought for a moment he had imagined it.

"Belinda?" He repeated and cleared his throat. He needed more gumption. More courage. *"Belinda, will you do the honor of being my wife? I asked your pa, and he gave me his blessing."*

She said nothing for a few seconds, and a crow cawed overhead. A gentle breeze rustled the canopy of trees above them. Perhaps he should have asked her to court him first. That was the natural way of things.

"I'm so sorry, Otis."

For a minute, he thought he might have misheard her. Doing as he always did when a challenging situation arose, he brought humor into it. *"I believe the answer would be yes?"* He offered his best smile.

She didn't return it like she usually did when he cracked one of his birdbrained jokes. Instead, a single tear slid down her cheek.

Had he been wrong in proposing? If there was one thing he never wanted to do, it was to make her upset. *"What is it? What's wrong?"*

"I'm so sorry, Otis," she said once again. She picked at a thread on her skirt. *"This isn't a good time."*

He didn't understand. It wasn't a good time to broach the subject? Or—*"What do you mean it isn't a good time? Not a good time to ask you to be my wife?"*

She nodded slowly, and his heart broke into four hundred million pieces.

"I can't marry you right now."

It wasn't as though they were sixteen years old, or even eighteen. They were mature adults. Why then? Did she wish to wait before agreeing? *"I'm not sure what you mean. If you want to wait a year or two or however long, I will wait for you, Belinda, for as long as it takes. Our courtship can be as lengthy as it needs to be."*

"No, it's not that." Another tear slid down her cheek and onto her skirt. He reached over and gently swiped away another as it emerged. She didn't flinch or back away, for which he was grateful.

Otis wasn't prone to impatience, but right then, he was feeling rather antsy. *"Then what is it?"*

Belinda hadn't answered. Instead, she stood, her legs wobbling. He stood as well and cupped her elbow to keep her from falling. Something was wrong.

Very wrong.

Why would she have this reaction to his question? Did she not feel the same? Why wasn't it a good time?

"Can you please take me home?"

"What did I do? What did I say to make you—"

But there was no answer because Belinda had already started walking toward the buggy.

Two weeks later, Belinda and her family moved to Hawthorne, to the ranch where her grandparents lived. Several days later, he discovered her grandparents had passed away, and her father sold their Hilltop ranch. He'd wanted to come alongside her and help her through the loss, but she kept her distance. He, Pa, and Mart assisted the Finnegans with their move. He didn't understand why Mr. Finnegan thought it wise to sell the thriving ranch in Hilltop, but Otis did his best to be as helpful as possible. Pa surmised it had to do with the fact that Mr. Finnegan had promised to take over the Hawthorne ranch someday after his parents died. Or perhaps it was because the Hawthorne ranch included twice as many acres. Whatever the reason, Otis and his family supported the Finnegans.

Otis had spent a considerable amount of time going over the entire day in his mind over and over again. If her reason for telling him it was not a good time was due to her grandparents' passing, why couldn't she have told him that? He would have understood. He would have been patient. He would have done whatever he could to alleviate her pain.

He would have waited.

CHAPTER SEVEN

Otis assisted Belinda into the sleigh. Today's bright and sunny weather was deceiving because the sun barely reached the earth to warm it. It had snowed last night, offering substantially more than a dusting.

He'd once again plopped Anne-Marie's green-and-beige hat on his head and wrapped the scarf Ma had made for him several Christmases ago around his neck, and steered the sleigh toward town. No words immediately came to mind, rendering an awkward silence between them.

The outskirts of Hawthorne appeared quite different in the daylight. Expansive ranches lined either side of the road. The Finnegans lived a short distance from town, and even now, Otis could see sparse buildings in the distance. He'd only visited the town a few times, and one of those times was when he, Pa, and Mart assisted Mr. Finnegan with moving all of their items from Hilltop. Otis hadn't completely understood the reason for the family's move, but he respected Belinda's father and knew the man had done what he felt was best for his family.

Otis attempted to keep his eyes on the road ahead

and not on his passenger. Belinda was as beautiful as he remembered, with her green eyes fringed with long lashes. Earlier that morning, he observed how pale she was and that she still seemed weak from the illness. From his side eye, he noticed her rosy cheeks, flushed from the biting wind.

"Are you warm enough?" He instinctively transferred the reins to one hand and tugged more of the quilt over her lap.

"I am, thank you."

Their gazes connected, and for a moment, he thought he might have seen the slight upturn of her lips into a smile. Even if they could rekindle their friendship, he would be—or at least attempt to be—satisfied with that. He could forgive her for breaking his heart, but he wasn't sure he could continue with them at such odds.

He cleared his throat. "Are you liking Hawthorne?"

"I am. However, I do miss Hilltop and my friends there."

Did she consider him a friend, and if so, among those friends she missed?

A rough-hewn piece of wood partially covered by snow indicated a population of 198. "Doc should be in his office. We can stop and ask him for his list of whom we can help deliver the medicines to. His office is right over there." Belinda pointed a mittened finger in the direction of a humble building with the shingle on the outside indicating it was the physician's office. The rest of the street was empty, and there were no lights on in any of the few businesses, except for the doctor's office and the bank.

Otis guided the horse to the right and parked directly in

front of Doc's. Once inside, Otis scanned the tight quarters that included a medical examination bed, potbellied stove, a mahogany desk with a matching chair, and a hefty hutch containing medical supplies and a few bottles and tins of medicine. Books and a pile of papers lined the desk. On the corner was a white bowl with a spoon and some oatmeal that Doc had likely forgotten about in his busy morning.

"I'm Otis MacCallum from Hilltop. I brought medicine and food. "

The doctor's squinty eyes widened. "You're an answer to prayer, young man. I'm Doc." He shook Otis's hand. "Good morning, Belinda. How is your family?"

"Ma's doing much better and is up and about. Leah and Ethel are there today, taking care of them. Mara is doing the same, and I fear Pa is worse."

Doc's furry brows knitted together. "I have several people to see today, but I will make it a point to also check on your father."

Belinda grasped the side of Doc's desk. Otis suggested she stay behind and allow him to deliver the items, but she wouldn't hear of it. That hadn't surprised him because Belinda was both charitable and stubborn. "Doc, would you mind if we carried in a few things and distributed them into crates? Belinda said the mercantile may have some we could use?"

"That sounds like an excellent idea. There isn't much room in here, so perhaps we should go over to the church instead. I'll meet you two there, as I need to first stop by Mr. and Mrs. Blackard's house—they are the mercantile owners—and see if they have some crates for us to borrow.

Our reverend is home ill as well, but I know he'll be amenable to us using the church."

The Hawthorne church was only a block away from Doc's. A small, white church with a tall steeple, it reminded Otis of the church in Hilltop, only half the size. Belinda stayed inside while Otis unloaded the supplies.

Doc arrived a few minutes later and said there were numerous crates available at the mercantile and that Otis and Belinda were welcome to use them. He then took several bottles and medicine tins to deliver on his rounds and handed Belinda a list of those who needed medicines the most.

The dispersing of the items went fairly quickly once they set the crates along the floor and placed a variety of food items into each one.

"Here are some trinkets from Mrs. Jowett's."

A genuine smile crossed Belinda's face. "From Mrs. Jowett's precious possessions?"

"Yes. You know how she loves to gift things from her attic to others. And she mentioned to me no less than four times that these were goods that the recipients could keep rather than borrow."

Otis set the box on the floor, and Belinda meandered over to it and removed several books. "I know just who would be so blessed by these." She held one of the books to her chest. "I remember reading this several times when I was in school."

The memories flooded through Otis's mind. He'd sat behind her in school that very first day when her family first moved to Hilltop. They'd become fast friends, and the teacher allowed him to move up to the desk beside her soon after. He'd made it his mission to find her books to borrow that she hadn't yet read—which was no easy task.

"Perhaps you can read it first before we pass it along."

Belinda held the book out in front of her, flipped through the pages, lifted it to her face, inhaled the ink, and nodded. "I always did love the smell of books. Or shall I say, the smell of adventure?"

The excitement in her countenance drew him to her, and for a moment, it was as though no time had passed between them. They were back in Hilltop, best friends as they'd always been. He realized he was staring, and with effort, averted his gaze to the mound of goods he still needed to unload.

"Yes, I think I shall borrow this one and then pass it along when I'm finished."

An hour later, they had filled most of the crates. Belinda removed a folded paper from her coat pocket. "Here is a list of the townsfolk. If we start on this end and work our way north, we should be able to deliver most of these fairly quickly. The homes to the west are more spread out, so that may take us a bit longer."

That was another thing he loved about her. She was a planner, always organized and reliable. Not in an overbearing way, but rather in a way that allowed others to know they could always fully depend on her. He doubted there was a time she'd ever let anyone down when they'd asked something of her. "I was just thinking about that time when the town decided we needed a Christmas play. You were instrumental in coordinating it, and as I recall, it was a huge success." He hoped Belinda could see the admiration in his eyes.

Belinda's tinkling laugh and now cheery disposition drew him all the more to her. "Oh, yes. I remember the Christmas play. From what I recall, word of it reached newspapers as far away as Bozeman, Missoula, and Helena, and maybe even parts of Idaho." A shadow briefly clouded her face. "I only wished I was able to…"

"Yes?"

"It's nothing."

Should he pry? There was a time when they shared nearly everything. Was she thinking of regrets about him? Or was the brief melancholy due to something else?

She moistened her lips. "I only wish I could have been as organized at home and caring for my family while they've been sick. I am quite concerned about Pa, especially. "

He wanted to put his arm around her and draw her to him and offer comfort. Instead, he prayed for the right words to say. "Your family is fortunate to have you to care for them. I know firsthand how challenging it can be to watch our loved ones struggle with sickness."

She chewed on her bottom lip. "Thank you."

The seconds ticked by as they sat there with no further words between them. Finally, Otis continued packing the remaining crates. "Shall we embark on our adventure?"

"Yes, I believe we shall."

The first several houses were close to town. At the fourth house, Belinda leaned across the sleigh and lowered her voice as if what she had to say was for his ears only.

"This is the one who will thoroughly enjoy several of those books from Mrs. Jowett."

Her legs faltered, and she quickly grasped the edge of the sleigh to steady herself, grateful that Otis's attention remained on unstrapping another crate. If Otis noticed she was not feeling her usual spry self, he'd insist she return home and allow him to deliver the food, medicine, and trinkets. He was one of the kindest and most thoughtful men she'd ever known, but while she would appreciate his concern, it was important to her to be able to make a difference and help those in need.

Once inside the whitewashed farmhouse and after introducing Otis to the four residents, Belinda asked her friend, Philippa, to close her eyes and hold out her hands.

Philippa's eyes revealed surprise, and she removed her arms, which had been tucked beneath a red-and-green Christmas quilt. She did as Belinda requested, and Belinda set three of Mrs. Jowett's books in her hands.

Philippa squealed, then sobered. "But I didn't get you a Christmas gift."

"Oh, these aren't for Christmas. These are from a dear friend in Hilltop. She loves to bless others with some of her possessions. When Otis brought these to Hawthorne, I knew the perfect person to give them to."

Philippa clutched the books to her chest. "Books always make things better. Please tell your friend thank you."

Otis assisted Philippa's mother and father with the items in the crate, and Philippa wiggled her finger at Belinda to lean closer. Belinda lowered herself to her knees and leaned toward her friend. "I have a question to ask of you, and I hope you won't mind terribly." Philippa and her family had moved from back East a couple of years ago, and Philippa had brought with her the propensity to use plentiful words in conversation when a few would do.

When Belinda moved to Hawthorne, she and Philippa, who was a year older, became fast friends. "Anything."

"Do you think there is a chance Glen might fancy me?"

Her friends' words were unexpected. "Oh."

Creases amassed on Philippa's forehead. "I mean to say that after this illness is over, I might perhaps enjoy spending time with Glen. But I don't want to be too forward, and I am uncertain what he thinks of me."

Belinda took a step back and perused the room. Philippas's parents were busy talking with Otis, and her younger brother was asleep on a nearby sofa. Guilt weighed on her. If Philippa fancied Glen, she couldn't let her know that Glen had asked Belinda to consider courtship with him. Did Glen cotton to Philippa at all? Likely not if he'd expressed interest in Belinda.

"Belinda?"

"Sorry. I was just considering your question."

"I do like him." Philippa smiled. "We talked overmuch at church several weeks ago. He's handsome, charming, kind, and of course, godly."

"Yes, he is."

"So, what do you think? Should I entertain such a

notion or am I merely being a foolhardy flibbertigibbet?"

Belinda shook her head. "I don't think you are a foolhardy flibbertigibbet at all. I don't know if Glen fancies you, but I'm sure if he does, he'll make his intentions known." Her words sounded flimsy in her own ears. She would speak with Glen soon and tell him she'd changed her mind about considering a courtship with him. Then Belinda would somehow weave Philippa's name into the conversation. Glen was an intelligent sort. Perhaps Belinda could even be a matchmaker.

"I do think he's positively dapper," added Philippa, whose pale face had taken on a rosy hue.

Belinda and Otis finished assisting Philippa's family before traveling to the next stop. As they rode around in the sleigh, she, for a moment, pretended as though things were perfectly fine between them. They had talked more about happenings in Hilltop, about Hawthorne, and about Tom, having to return to work at the bank even though there were few, if any, customers. As they conversed, Belinda was reminded of how easy Otis was to talk to.

They stopped around noon and returned to the church, where the pastor's wife, who had recently recovered, brought them some sandwiches. They then started toward the western part of the town. Exhaustion overcame Belinda, and she closed her eyes for a few minutes, the sleigh lulling her into a calming peace until she awoke to a gentle nudging from Otis. "Is this house on our list?" Belinda opened her eyes and looked out over the white fields to a yellow farmhouse with a white-railed porch that wrapped around the front and part of one side.

"Yes, this is one of our stops." She must have slept for quite a while because the Hiatt home was two miles from town.

Otis parked and proceeded to assist her from the sleigh. Her legs nearly toppled out from beneath her, and she fell into his arms. For a few seconds, she rested there, relishing the strength of his embrace and the comfort she'd missed. Her head fit perfectly below his chin, and he smelled of pine. Her heart fluttered, and she rested against his chest, briefly forgetting the discord between them.

CHAPTER EIGHT

OTIS HELD BELINDA IN his arms. Could she hear the pounding of his heart through his thick winter coat?

If he had been asked even as recently as yesterday whether he thought he would ever be spending time with Belinda again, let alone see her, he would have said no. Yet here he was standing in the cold on a wintry day in December with her firmly in his arms. Thoughts of the past and how she declined his offer for courtship melted away, replaced by a sprig of hope. If he could hold her every day for the rest of their lives, it wouldn't be often enough.

You, Otis, are a lovestruck fool.

Yes, he was a lovestruck fool. And he'd hold on to any ounce of hope that there was a future for them.

She pulled away first and tilted her head back. Her eyes met his.

"Otis..."

The door of the farmhouse creaked open. "Belinda, is that you?"

A tall woman with blonde hair stood on the porch, framing her face with her hand and squinting into the sun toward Otis and Belinda.

"Yes, Mrs. Hiatt, it's me. We came to deliver some food and some medicine. "

"I am so happy to hear that. Please do come in."

Otis had already noticed Belinda's exhaustion. "You go ahead. I can get the crate."

"They will need two crates."

Otis carried one crate, then the second, into the warm house where several children rested in the parlor, the living room, and, from the sounds of coughing, upstairs as well. Belinda introduced him to Mr. and Mrs. Hiatt. Mrs. Hiatt looked to be on the mend, but Mr. Hiatt, his face gaunt and with his sharp barking cough, still struggled with the illness.

After visiting the Hiatts, Belinda told him there were only two more places left to go. Thankfully, Doc had taken a number of the crates on his rounds. Otis glanced up at the sky. The sun would soon be setting, and already the temperature had dropped significantly from just hours before. He would need to get Belinda home as soon as possible, and then perhaps he could deliver the other supplies by himself tomorrow. He once again assisted her into the sleigh, and they drove in the direction of Belinda's house. "The other two are on the way."

"I can deliver the crates tomorrow."

Indecision flashed in her eyes. "I may agree on one of them, but the other one—"

"If you're sure. I could even deliver the crate myself."

He knew even as he said it that Belinda would prefer not to stay in the sleigh while he carried the supplies to the front door. Belinda enjoyed visiting with the other townsfolk, many of whom she considered friends.

"I think I will be fine, but thank you all the same. And thank you, Otis, for being so willing to drive all this way and to deliver the food and medicine."

"You're welcome."

He turned his attention from the road. She met his gaze and held it once again. "Otis…"

"Yes?"

"There's something I need to tell you."

His heart drummed up several notches. "Yes?" He held his breath. Whatever it was she wished to say, he wanted to hear it.

"Oh, no! We just drove right past Glen's parents' house."

Otis had no idea who Glen was, but clearly, Glen's home was a place they needed to visit. He pulled on the reins and promptly reversed direction and headed back to a two-story white house next to a large red barn.

He was about to ask what it was she needed to tell him when she pointed at the house. "It looks as though no one has been outside today."

The worried tone in her voice caused him to decline asking her about their unfinished conversation. He sought to reassure her. "I can shovel a pathway for them from the house to the barn. "

The way she looked at him with such gratitude made him want to shovel a pathway all the way from Hawthorne to Hilltop.

"Thank you. I think they would appreciate that."

He parked the sleigh and they trudged through the snow to the front door. After Belinda knocked, a slim man with reddish hair about their age answered. "Belinda, it's so nice to see you." The man ushered them both inside.

"Glen, this is my friend from Hilltop, Otis. Otis, this is Glen." She directed her attention to Glen. "How is your family doing?"

"Everyone is feeling much better, but we stayed in today."

"I'm glad that's all it was. I was concerned when I didn't see any tracks in the snow."

Glen nodded. "I stayed here last night and tended to chores before it snowed again early this morning."

Belinda and Glen continued to converse, and Otis offered to shovel a path to the barn and check on the animals.

Glen's pa thanked him, but Otis wasn't sure that Belinda or Glen heard Otis's offer. They were absorbed in conversation, and something about the way Glen looked at Belinda reminded Otis of a man who considered her more than a friend. Affection was clearly written in the man's eyes.

Not that Otis was jealous. Or maybe he was just a smidgeon. Jealous that perhaps Belinda fancied Glen, and Otis had lost his one chance to win her heart.

A thought niggled him deep in the gut. What if Belinda felt for Glen what he likely felt for her? What if the feeling was mutual? He swallowed past the squeeze in his throat. Above all else, Otis would want Belinda to be happy, even if she ultimately would not choose him.

He shoveled a pathway faster than usual, attempting to keep himself warm. The breeze had picked up, and from the sky's appearance, more snow was imminent. He opened the barn door, checked inside, then returned to the house. Belinda and Glen were standing near the table, still immersed in conversation.

He'd been foolish to think there was a possibility for them after all this time.

Belinda dreaded the conversation she needed to have with Glen. She'd already broken one heart, and she didn't wish to break another. Glen was a kindly fellow, and he and Philippa would be a delightful match. The challenge was to somehow convince him, without disappointing him, that she would no longer be considering his request for courtship.

At least Glen had always been easy to talk to in the time she'd known him, although they didn't share the easy camaraderie she and Otis did.

Despite praying for the opportunity to somehow talk with Glen about the pending courtship, Belinda was not given the opportunity. Instead, they discussed their families' illnesses, the new horse Glen hoped to purchase in the spring, and the tragedy of losing some of the townsfolk. Glen mentioned that Mr. Hibbard, the cantankerous older gentleman who lived by himself next to the livery, had died after a valiant fight against pneumonia last night. "Doc said his coughs, fever, and chest pain wouldn't relent. Despite prayers and Doc's best efforts..."

Glen needn't continue. Belinda knew this ruthless sickness had already claimed so many lives—even one life was too many. She hoped that having enough medicine and food would now improve the chances of recovery for the remaining townsfolk.

She and Otis left a short time later. She snuggled beneath the extra blankets in the sleigh and closed her eyes. The day had exhausted her, but at the same time, the ability to help others invigorated her.

Her thoughts turned to Otis and how she desperately wanted to apologize to him, but the timing had not yet been right. Perhaps tomorrow. She knew he would have to leave for Hilltop, and she didn't want any more unspoken words about the day he proposed to persist between them.

She was dreaming about summer and riding a train to Helena when she felt a gentle nudge on her arm.

"Belinda? We're home."

She hadn't heard the conductor announce they were stopping soon. She blinked, then nestled herself back against the seat once again. Perhaps she was still dreaming. After all, the train ride had been lengthy. Confusion reigned, and she attempted to recall where she was and why. Belinda fluttered her eyes, willing them to open. Why was her neck cramped? She shifted, closed her eyes again, then opened them to see Otis's face before her. *Otis?* No, she definitely was not on the train.

"Belinda? We're home," he repeated.

She reached up with a mittened hand and wiped the sleep from her eyes. The ride from Glen's parents' house to hers wasn't far, but she had slept soundly during that time. She yawned and sat up straighter in the sleigh. A rush of bitterly cold air assaulted her, and she shivered. Otis assisted her from the sleigh and to the front door. "I'm going to unhitch the horse. I'll be in in a minute."

Belinda entered the house, a slew of warm air welcoming her. It was late, and Leah had already gone home. She closed the door behind her, but kept her coat on for a few more minutes as she allowed the heat from the house to seep into her cold bones. She walked to the fireplace and held her hands above the smoldering embers. She would need to light the fire again if they were to remain warm throughout the night.

"Belinda, is that you?"

"Yes, Ma. How is everyone?"

At that moment, a loud, deep, hacking, persistent cough emanated through the quietness. Ma shuffled away and toward her and Pa's room. Belinda hastily removed her coat, tossed it on the sofa, and urged her lethargic self up the stairs. Ma emerged from her room, nearly colliding with Belinda. Her mother's voice rose several octaves in panic. "Something isn't right. Pa is complaining of his chest hurting, and he's violently shaking."

Pa continued to cough, and Belinda traipsed through the doorway to find him curled in a ball, his body indeed, as Ma had mentioned, violently shaking. He had coughed into a handkerchief, and when Belinda looked down at it, she noticed thick, yellowish-green mucus.

Dread filled every part of her. The room swirled as dizziness took hold, and her legs shook, although this time not from the weakness of her recovering illness. "We have to fetch Doc."

Ma had fallen to her knees and had wrapped her arms around Pa, holding him to her and gently rocking him while beseeching that the Lord heal her husband.

From the other room, Mara called out, her voice hoarse. "Belinda? Is Pa all right?"

Belinda's feet were anchored to the floor, and her heart palpitated. She needed to leave the room and find Otis, but she couldn't move. Why did her legs feel so heavy? She struggled to lift them. Thoughts of Mr. Hibbard filled her mind. Did Pa have pneumonia as well?

Lord, please, help Pa. Belinda closed her eyes, gripped the doorknob, and prayed that God would give her the strength to do what needed to be done. Then, with effort, she shifted first her right foot in front of her left and trudged to the top of the stairs. In a blurred haze, she heard Mara call out again. She needed to reassure her younger sister. Staggering to the open door, she leaned her head in. "Everything will be all right." But even in her own mind, Belinda wasn't so sure.

In a fog, she somehow made it down the stairs and out the front door. It was there that she collided with Otis.

"Belinda?" He placed his hands on her shoulders.

"Otis, we need to fetch Doc. Pa isn't well." Her voice wavered, and she hoped he could understand the gibberish. She sank into his arms and rested her head briefly on his muscled chest, finding solace there for the second time today.

She needed to retreat from the comfort of his embrace and allow him to go to town. Finally, Otis took a step back and lifted her chin with his finger. "I am going to go fetch Doc. I need you to keep an eye on your family until I get back."

She nodded mutely and staggered back inside.

At the window, she watched as Otis disappeared into the night. Mara called out again, and Pa's coughs resumed.

She needed to be strong for her family.

Belinda heated some broth, then took it, a pitcher of water, some cinnamon, and garlic, and plodded up the stairs. She stopped by her and Mara's room and fumbled to remove the quilt from her bed, then ambled into Ma and Pa's room. Thankful for God's grace in giving her the strength to do what needed to be done, Belinda aided Ma with making Pa more comfortable, spoon feeding him some broth, adding cinnamon and garlic, and wrapping the blanket firmly around him. Pa moaned about the chest pain.

Ma continued feeding Pa while Belinda checked on Mara. "My legs and arms hurt and my neck too," whispered her younger sister.

"I know, sweetie, I know. It's all part of this illness."

"Can I go see Pa?"

Belinda smoothed her sister's blonde hair from her forehead. "I'm sorry, but no. It's best you stay here. How about some water?"

Mara shook her head. "I'm not thirsty, and it hurts to swallow."

"You have to have something to drink."

Mara's lips were chapped, and the skin on her face and hands was so dry. Belinda assisted Mara into a sitting position, then lifted the cup of water to her sister's lips.

In a haphazard fashion that left most of the water dribbling down her chin, Mara drank the tiniest of sips before plunging back down again on her pillow.

Belinda measured some Dover's Powder from the dresser beside Mara's bed and fed it to her sister. Cow climbed up into the bed and nuzzled against Mara, and Belinda retreated to her parents' room. Her mother, despite her own frailty, was doing remarkably well tending to Pa. Belinda hastened downstairs for more broth and fed it to a hesitant Mara.

Her sister was only able to eat a small portion, but Belinda would be content with whatever Mara could ingest.

When would Doc arrive? Was Otis able to find him? He knew where the office was, but Belinda failed in her stupor to tell him where Doc lived.

The minutes seemed to pass slowly, even though she was far from idle in continually caring for her family.

CHAPTER NINE

OTIS URGED HIS HORSE forward, his eyes straining to see a few feet ahead of him. The look on Belinda's face devastated him. He would do just about anything for her. The frosty air numbed his cheeks, and he wiggled his frozen toes in his boots. Was it his imagination, or did his horse resist clomping through the deep snow? "I know it's cold, girl, and you'd rather be in the barn." He patted her head, and she neighed and snorted in response.

The ride to town took an eternity. Twice, Otis wondered if he was even going in the right direction. Few lights shone, stars were absent, and an unwavering assembly of clouds eerily skittered across the moon, foretelling another snowstorm. Murky shadows hovered along the side of the road. Was he even *still* on the road? In daylight, he could discern a shortcut, but not in the gloominess of the night.

Lord, please guide my way. It wouldn't do to become lost and stranded. Not when Mr. Finnegan desperately needed Doc's help.

Snowflakes pelted Otis's face, and he squinted. A light to the left offered encouragement and reminded him he'd not strayed too far from the path. He forged ahead, soon losing track of time, the endless road to town infinite and daunting. An owl hooted, a coyote howled, and the rush of a gust of wind surged through the trees.

Weariness weighed on him. He blinked, attempting to keep his eyes open.

Another light shone ahead at the top of the hill. If he was correct in his assumptions, Hawthorne lay just beyond.

Climbing the hill took longer than he remembered as his horse plodded along much more slowly than Otis preferred. Otis's thoughts reverted again to Belinda. She'd been diligent in taking care of her family. Dedicated to caring for those whom she loved. Earnest in seeing to it that the townsfolk received the necessary food and medicine. He appreciated her strength and fortitude.

He edged his way up the sloped terrain. Its incline was far less arduous than the route from Hilltop to the ranch. When he reached the top, lights flickered below, indicating he'd reached Hawthorne. He released a bottled sigh, feeling somewhat victorious.

Otis stopped first at Doc's office. There were no lights on, but he knocked just in case. When there was no answer, he hung his head briefly, but just as quickly, resisted the urge to give in to defeat. He strolled down the snow and ice-covered boardwalk in search of a business with lights—somewhere where he could ask where Doc's home was.

The mercantile was completely dark, but upstairs a light flickered in the window. There was no way to access the upstairs from the front of the building, but if he were to hazard a guess, there would be a back entrance with a tall staircase just like at the mercantile in Hilltop.

He mounted his horse and turned the corner at the end of the block. Snow had drifted in between the buildings, some of those drifts as tall as four to five feet. Otis examined the two-story buildings. From this angle, there were no lights on at all, not even where he surmised the mercantile to be. Should he travel further to the outskirts of town and ask at one of the houses he'd already passed? Or should he climb one of the staircases and knock on the door?

Prayer for wisdom was in order.

Otis decided to ascend the stairs at the back of the mercantile. He once again tethered his horse and waded it through the drifts to a narrowly shoveled pathway. Snow seeped into his boots, freezing his lower legs and feet. Gripping the railing, he started up the stairs but slipped on the fourth one. He fell, his shin connecting hard with the wood. He groaned and forced himself upright again. Five steps later, he reached the top. He knocked on the door and waited. The floor creaked, indicating movement inside. He knocked again. Likely, the resident wasn't expecting someone to visit at this late hour.

"Who is it?"

"I'm hoping you can help me find Doc." The door opened about six inches, and a frail woman stood to the side and motioned him in.

The smell of sickness permeated the air. He fought the bile that rose in his throat even as he recognized the odor from when his own family was sick and from staying at the Finnegans'.

"Have you been to his house?"

"I'm afraid I don't know where he lives. I'm staying with the Finnegan family, and Mr. Finnegan has taken a turn for the worse."

Lines creased the woman's already wrinkled face. "I am so sorry to hear that. Doc was by here earlier because my husband and daughter haven't healed as quickly as we'd like. If you go back outside and turn right at the end of the block, you'll eventually come to a brown house on the corner. I know it's hard to see with all the snow, but you probably can't miss it—it's a more elaborate home than most in this area. You'll take a left turn at that corner until you reach a white house with a sprawling porch. That's Doc's house. If you arrive at the livery, you've gone too far."

"Thank you very much, ma'am, for your help.

"You're welcome, and please tell the Finnegans I'll be praying for them."

Otis limped out the door and gripped the railing more firmly this time as he descended the stairs. The wind had picked up, and swirls of snow smoothed over his footprints.

Five minutes later, he came to the white house with a sprawling front porch. Fortunately, there was a light on inside. *Thank you, Lord.*

At his knock, Doc swung the door open. "Otis, what can I do for you?"

"Mr. Finnegan has taken a turn for the worse. Belinda fears it might be pneumonia."

A woman with a red-and-yellow apron stepped from the kitchen area. She and Doc said their goodbyes, and Doc planted a kiss on her forehead. "I may have to stay the night."

His wife nodded. "I love you. Please be careful."

Otis turned away to give them some privacy before he and Doc left the home and started again toward the Finnegan ranch.

Belinda stood in the doorway as Doc tended to Pa. Ma sat in the chair at the end of the bed. Pa had barely moved in the last little while, except when the coughs racked his body, which took what little energy he had left. Or when he began shaking and sweating profusely.

Doc removed the thermometer from Pa's mouth. "He's burning with fever."

Pa had frequently complained of chest pain, and his wheezing indicated shortness of breath. In the last hour, her father had also vomited, and the cough produced a plethora of green mucus in his handkerchief. Belinda didn't need to see Doc's face to know how serious it was, and she offered her thousandth prayer.

"He does have pneumonia," said Doc.

Both Belinda and Ma gasped in tandem.

Ma gripped Pa's hand. "What can be done?"

Doc pushed up the sleeves of his shirt. "Much can be done. First, we need to prepare a poultice for the lung fever. Do you have any onions and rye flour?”

“Yes, we do,” said Ma.

The physician dictated the directions, and Ma and Belinda set to work downstairs. Ma grabbed the table to steady herself. Her lip trembled. “I love him so much, Belinda. I can’t lose him.”

“I know, Ma.” She wanted to be strong for her mother, but the concerns weaved their way through her mind with an unrelenting force. She hugged Ma. “I’m going to keep praying he’ll be all right.”

Ma blinked, her eyes swimming with tears. “I am going to have faith that he will be.”

Belinda would do her best to believe that as well. She again hugged Ma, grateful the Lord had blessed her with such a loving mother.

Doc prescribed a lukewarm bath to address Pa’s fever as well as more Dover’s Powder for the pain. “We can also try Chamberlain’s Cough Remedy. I’ll leave some of that here as well. The dosage is a teaspoonful for your father, but since Mara is only fifteen, give her three-fourths of a teaspoon.” Then, while Doc and Ma tended to Pa’s bath, Belinda again checked on Mara.

Her sister had fallen asleep, her blonde hair plastered to her forehead. Mara’s fever had broken earlier today. Belinda rested a hand on her sister’s arm. “Lord, thank You for the healing You have already done in Ma, Mara, Leah, Tom, Ethel, and me. Please continue to heal everyone fully, and please help Pa. Please don’t let us lose him.” She released Mara’s arm, and her sister stirred slightly. Belinda rose, and on tired legs, started down the stairs, a mixture of emotions flooding through her and the tears streaming down her face. Trepidation about Pa's condition, Ma still being so weak, Mara having lost so much weight, and the concern that Belinda herself was not here during the day to assist with Pa. Would it have made any difference if she had been?

Belinda released a shaky breath. At least she'd been able to tell Pa she loved him earlier today and again before leaving his and Ma's room, but if something happened to him...

She threw another log on the fireplace. The door creaked open, and Otis strolled in. Without a second thought, she hurried toward him. He opened his arms and she fell into his embrace, relishing the comfort she found there, the tears flowing freely. She ought to allow him to at least remove his coat and hat. Belinda took a step back. "I'm sorry."

His eyes searched her face. "You have nothing to be sorry for."

"I know you would like to remove your coat and hat." She looked up and saw snow caked to his thick eyelashes. The cold emanated from him. What he must have gone through to fetch Doc...her respect, admiration, and love grew for him.

Otis unbuttoned his coat, unwound his scarf, and removed his hat. She offered to take the clothing from him and set it on the chair at the table.

"Thank you so much for fetching Doc."

He opened his arms again. She needed no prompting.

Otis held Belinda tight. She felt good in his arms. Like she belonged there—and he wished that she did. But no matter her rejection of his marriage proposal, he would always be there for her as her friend, no matter what. Even if he wished it could be more.

He kissed the top of her head and gently rubbed her back. The sobs wracked her body. He wanted to ask about her father, but for now, he would just hold her. His own eyes smarted with emotion. He didn't know what it was like to lose someone, but he did know what it was like to love your family and cherish them and to come close to losing someone. He knew Belinda was exceptionally close to her parents and sisters, just like he was with his parents, siblings, and grandparents.

After a few minutes, she slowly stepped back. "I am so thankful Doc arrived. Thank you."

"You're welcome." He would omit telling her he'd almost not been successful. "How is your pa doing?"

"Doc confirmed he does have pneumonia." Belinda's watery gaze settled on something in the distance. Her eyebrows drew together, and the dark circles beneath her eyes told of her lack of sleep. "What if Pa doesn't make it?"

He didn't know what to say in response to her question. He recalled some of the folks who had lost their lives to influenza and pneumonia in Hilltop. It hadn't necessarily been the weakest or the oldest. Even one child, a formerly healthy older boy three years younger than Anne-Marie, lost his life. Another, a man in his early forties, had also died. "We must keep praying."

She nodded and rubbed the side of her neck. "I know Pa will be with Jesus if he dies, but I am not ready to let him go, and I can't even imagine Ma losing him."

A flashback of his grandfather barely clinging to life entered Otis's mind. His elderly grandpa almost didn't make it through the illness. Otis's throat closed up for a minute as he recalled that day. "I remember feeling so helpless when Grandpa was at his sickest. He had been brought down to rest on the sofa. For the longest time, he barely moved. Grandma was beside herself, and the rest of us were in the early stages of the sickness. I remember forcing my legs to carry me to the sofa. I sat down on a chair beside Grandpa and reached for his hand. His eyes fluttered open, and he told me how thankful he was to have me for a grandson, and that he loved me from the first day he'd met me." Otis's own vision blurred slightly as he fought to contain his sorrow.

"That must have been so hard."

"It was. We weren't sure for the longest time." He didn't add that Grandpa had been far from frail, although he was old. Mr. Finnegan wasn't frail either.

"I'm so grateful God healed him."

"As am I. Would you like to pray again for your pa?"

When Belinda slowly nodded, Otis lifted another prayer for Mr. Finnegan. He added a request for peace and comfort for Belinda, her mother, and Mara, and for the wisdom for Doc to know how to treat the pneumonia.

"Thank you, Otis."

He held her again, allowing her to nestle against his chest for as long as she needed. He hoped it wasn't the Lord's will that Mr. Finnegan would not recover. But if it was, he would be there for Belinda and her family.

Doc called to them, and Belinda rushed to the stairs. As she did so, Otis immediately missed holding her. He limped to the sofa and removed his shoes. His socks were drenched, and his feet and lower legs were red and burning. He lifted his pant leg and saw the bruise forming on his shin along with a nasty scrape. He quickly covered it again and figured he'd best change out of his wet pants. Then he'd need to go upstairs and see if he could offer any assistance.

"Otis? What happened?"

He hadn't noticed that she had returned.

"Snow got inside my boots. How is your pa?"

"His fever is still so high."

"I'm sorry, Belinda."

"Doc says it's going to be a long night."

The physician walked down the stairs and toward them. "I'll be staying throughout the night and tending to your father. I've encouraged your mother to move into your and Mara's room."

"I'm not sure I can sleep," said Belinda.

Doc rested a hand on Belinda's shoulder. "Lest you suffer a relapse, it's best you get your rest."

"But if something happens..."

This time, it was Otis who provided comfort through a hand on her arm. "Belinda..."

"No, I can't just go to sleep. If something happens to Pa, and I could have been awake to help—"

"There's nothing you can do." Doc furrowed his brow. "I have some other things to try in an attempt to reduce his fever, and I've been able to convince him to take small sips of water to alleviate the dehydration. The poultice is intended to help with the pneumonia. If there is any change, I'll let you know."

"Do you think he'll pull through?"

Doc didn't need to say anything; the answer was written on his weathered face.

Belinda searched Doc's gaze. "Please, Doc, tell us the truth."

"We will do everything we can to ensure your father heals. Continue to pray for his recovery, as I know you have been. Pray for me for guidance and wisdom as I treat your father. Many, many have survived pneumonia. I know it will be arduous, but do return upstairs as soon as you can and get some shuteye. It won't do to have you take ill with the lung fever as well. You, too, Otis."

"Yes, sir," Otis answered.

Doc nodded and returned upstairs. Otis and Belinda stood in the silence of the room with only the ticking of the clock, the muffled voices, and Mr. Finnegan's deep cough and labored breathing upstairs. Otis might as well say what was on his mind. "Belinda, there's something I need to discuss with you."

"There's something I need to tell you as well." A single tear slid down her cheek.

Otis nodded in agreement. He knew Belinda would

likely disagree with his suggestion, but it was necessary. "Seeing as how your father is so ill, I'm going to stay longer and help with the chores."

Belinda's jaw dropped. "We can't ask you to do that, Otis."

"You don't have to ask me. I'm offering."

"But it's almost Christmas. You should be home with your family." Her voice broke.

Yes, he would miss his family, and this would be the first year they would celebrate Christmas without him, but he couldn't just leave the Finnegans to fend for themselves with Mr. Finnegan being so sick, Tom having to work at the bank, and Belinda and her ma barely able to keep up with the household chores. Yesterday, when he'd visited with the hired hand, the man had coughed and complained of various aches and pains. Otis figured it wouldn't be long before he succumbed to the illness as well. "I plan to stay here as long as you need me." He hoped the finality in his voice persuaded her that this was imperative. He knew that Mr. Finnegan, just as any rancher did, feared losing all he'd worked so hard for.

Belinda's shoulders slumped. "I can't say it wouldn't be appreciated, but I really don't want you to have to be away from your family."

He reached for her hand. To his relief, she didn't resist. "Tomorrow I will venture into town and send a telegram. I've been wanting to check on my family and see how they're doing, anyhow. I'll let them know my plans."

"When you decided to come to Hawthorne, you didn't anticipate having to stay this long. I truly appreciate it, and

I know my parents will too."

"I'm happy to do it." The fireplace flames danced on the wall, illuminating a frail Belinda. She was normally so strong and capable, but today, with her shoulders bowed, her sagging posture, and her head lowered, defeat overwhelmed her countenance. "Belinda."

She once again collapsed into him. "What if Pa doesn't make it?"

Her muffled question with her face buried in his chest caused Otis to once seek the Lord's guidance. What if Mr. Finnegan *didn't* survive the lung fever? Otis knew without a doubt that he and his family would do whatever was necessary to provide for the Finnegan family. Still, that reassurance wouldn't make it any easier for Belinda to lose the father she loved, and Mrs. Finnegan to lose her husband.

Otis gently rubbed her arms. "I know you love your pa, but we have to put him in the Lord's hands."

"I know that, it's just I couldn't bear the thought..." Her words drifted. "I know we ought not borrow worries, but he's so feeble and sickly. I've never seen him look the way he does now. He's always been healthy, hearty, and resilient. I don't ever recall a time when he was ill before now." She choked a sob, and he pulled her closer.

"It's hard to see someone we love so ill, but, Belinda, you have to give this to the Lord."

"I have been praying. It seems God is silent."

"Not silent. Working things according to His will."

"But what if His will is to take Pa Home?"

"I pray it's not His will, but if it is, God will be by your family's side through it all. He tells us in His Word that He never leaves us or forsakes us."

She nuzzled into his chest, her body trembling. "You're right, it's just worrisome."

"Of course it is. This is your pa."

"Thank you for being here. For staying and helping."

"You're welcome." If only she could know the depth of his love for her. That Otis wanted to be there through the good times and bad. To share a life with her.

He brushed the thoughts aside and watched her as she padded up the steps. Staying and helping was such a small thing, and he'd happily do it. Otis kept the fire stoked throughout the night, and twice, he wandered upstairs to see if Doc needed any assistance.

Silly Cow slept through the whole thing.

Otis rode into town the following day to send a telegram to Ma and Pa. Mr. Finnegan had a grueling night, and there were times Otis worried the man would surrender to the fight. Finally, at two in the afternoon the following day, after a bath and capsicum slightly lowered Mr. Finnegan's fever, and he'd fallen asleep for some much-needed rest, Doc indicated Mr. Finnegan had survived the worst.

He would pull through.

Otis thanked the Lord no less than fifty times on his ride through the deep snow. He stopped at the post office, visited with the clerk who had reopened just two days ago, and sent his telegram letting his parents know of his plans and asking how everyone fared. He hoped they were able to respond soon.

The mercantile opened for the first time in days, and someone had placed some festive decorations in the window. It didn't quite seem like Christmas this year. Perhaps Otis could change that.

CHAPTER TEN

PA HAD IMPROVED GREATLY. Ma and Belinda continued the treatment Doc prescribed, and the physician had left by late afternoon and returned again the next day to check on Pa's progress. Mara had managed a few steps today and had eaten an entire bowl of soup.

The Lord was good.

At the beginning of the year, Ma hung up the calendar on the wall near the kitchen cupboards. A picture of St. Nick, with a basket strapped to his back full of toys, as he meandered through a scene of snow, represented the month of December. The bright, vibrant red, green, and white colors and layering of holly berries made the calendar far too lovely to discard after 1906 ended.

This year, Christmas fell on a Tuesday, just a couple of days away. It wouldn't be the typical Christmas this year without the Nativity scene carved by Grandpa, a tree, Ma's cinnamon rolls, shopping at the mercantile with Leah, or Pa playing Christmas songs on his harmonica, but it would be the best Christmas because her family would still be together after an especially harrowing December.

No, it didn't seem like the usual Christmas, but perhaps

Belinda could change that.

She anticipated Otis's return from town. Several times over the past few days, she had attempted to discuss with him the day that she declined his proposal, to no avail. Hopefully, she would have another chance this evening.

While Ma tended to Pa, Belinda prepared the noonday meal. Although she had spent many Christmas seasons at Otis's house with her entire family and attended Christmas Eve services at the Hilltop church, this was the first year in Hawthorne. Different still was the fact that Otis would be celebrating with them. A small niggle of worry crept into her mind. It didn't seem fair that he should miss time with his own family, but with Pa unable to handle chores and their only healthy hired hand now terribly ill, Belinda was beyond thankful for Otis's offer.

She'd noticed a hole in the leg of his pants last night. Today, she had arisen early and patched the hole. Perhaps later, she could ride to town if all was well, and meet with Leah at the mercantile. She wanted to be able to purchase her family some gifts, and she had just the thing in mind for Otis.

A knock at the door interrupted her musings, and when she opened it, she saw Glen standing on the sunny porch. She motioned him inside.

"How is your pa?"

She appreciated Glen's thoughtfulness and concern for her father. His generous spirit would make it all the harder to tell him what she must say. "He's doing better. And your family?"

"Much better, praise God." Glen fidgeted and shuffled

his feet. "Do you have a moment to discuss something?"

Did he and his family need more food? If so, Belinda would happily pootle down to the cellar and retrieve whatever they needed. "Absolutely. As a matter of fact, I wish to discuss something with you as well." Glen's timing couldn't be better. Belinda thought of what Philippa had said as she looked into her neighbor's kind eyes. She wanted to do nothing to hurt him, and she prayed for the right words to say and to say them in God's perfect timing.

She offered Glen a glass of water. He paced the floor before settling again near the table. Something was clearly bothering him. She was about to ask when he spoke.

"I didn't sleep well thinking about this last night," he began.

Glen was a nervous sort. "If it's about more food..."

"It's not about food. We have plenty, and we're much obliged for you delivering more the other day." He paused and threaded his fingers through his thick reddish hair. "I don't really know how to say this—"

Belinda waited patiently. "Yes?"

"I realize I said the other day that after all this was over, I would like to court you, and would you consider it."

"I remember." Once Glen said what was on his mind, she would need to tell him her thoughts.

"You know that I value our friendship and I would never want to do anything to purposely upset you."

"Yes, and I feel the same." How could she tell Glen that she was not interested in courting him, but knew someone who was?

Glen picked a thread on his coat. "I will have to rescind

my offer."

"Oh?"

His voice lowered to a barely audible tone. "I have feelings for someone else."

Belinda covered her mouth with her hand.

Glen took a step toward her, his brows knitted in concern. "Belinda, I am so sorry. I should never have asked to court you when there was someone else I fancied. I never realized there might be a chance with her. I'm usually not such a dullard. Can you forgive me?"

"I am actually glad we are discussing this." Her only concern now was gently telling Philippa that Glen cottoned to someone else.

"You are? I'm afraid I don't understand."

"I visited a friend while Otis and I were delivering medicine and food, and she told me she was fond of you. Because you asked me to consider courting you, I wasn't sure what to do. She and I are close friends, and I would never want anything to threaten that friendship. I regret to say that my feelings for you don't extend beyond friendship. From what you mentioned, you feel the same."

"That is true, and I'm so thankful you understand. But I must ask, who is this other woman?"

"I'm not sure I should say until I discuss with her these latest developments."

Glen rubbed his chin. "That sounds fair."

"Might I ask whom you fancy?"

"Yes. It's Philippa."

Belinda's eyes widened, and she gasped. "Philippa?"

A broad smile covered Glen's face. "Yes, Philippa."

Belinda shared with him about her discussion with her friend yesterday, and together, she and Glen chuckled at the irony.

After Glen left several minutes later, Belinda pondered a thought—if only her discussion with Otis could be resolved as easily.

Otis arrived an hour later. "It smells delicious in here," he exclaimed. "Almost reminds me of Mrs. Stroud's famous Christmas plum pudding pie."

"I do remember that. That is probably one of my favorite dishes that she makes, but no, it's not plum pudding pie, although I was considering making a mince pie." Then a thought struck her. While she didn't have the gift of cooking and baking like Mrs. Stroud did, perhaps she could bake a plum pudding pie as part of Christmas dinner as a surprise for Otis.

Otis hoped Belinda would find his idea a grand one. The sun was shining brightly outside, the air was warmer than it had been in recent days, and there wasn't much time. After he asked how her family fared, he asked if she might be able to leave for a few moments.

"I must admit curiosity has bested me. I think Ma would be able to handle it for a short while. Where would we go?"

"That is for me to know and for you to wonder." He offered his best smile. It was a line his family used often when they were about to surprise each other. "After the noonday meal, I would request your presence in the sleigh." He bowed and extended a hand toward her.

Belinda giggled. He'd missed the sweet sound of her laugh. She accepted his hand and feigned a British accent. "I do believe, perchance, that I might be able to accompany you on such a journey."

"Very well then. We shall plan on it for certain."

Were it anyone else, Otis wouldn't even consider acting as though he were a British lord, but with Belinda...

With Belinda, things were different. Theirs was a relationship he treasured. The thought of what had happened last spring entered his mind, and he shoved it aside. He didn't want anything to ruin this moment between them. So instead, he spun her around as though they were at a dance. They had attended several of those over the years in Hilltop in his parents' oversized barn, and for a moment, he pretended he was back there again, dancing with Belinda to their hearts' content, drinking punch, eating cookies, and talking about anything and everything.

He couldn't wait to surprise her with his plan. After he spun her a couple of times, he stopped and stared into her eyes. A dab of flour rested on her chin, and he tenderly swiped it away. His breath caught. Oh, but to hold her each day. To love her. To spend his life with her.

Was he a romantic sort? He would say no, but right now, he could likely argue that point with himself. He leaned toward her, his gaze resting on her full lips. He wouldn't deny that he wanted to kiss her. To twirl her around in his arms and kiss her again. He sucked in a breath. So much was uncertain, and he had no idea if she felt for him the way he felt for her.

The last thing he needed was a twice-over broken heart by the same woman.

An hour later, after the noonday meal and after Belinda reassured herself that her ma would be fine caring for her pa and Mara, Otis assisted her into the sleigh. There were chores to do, but this took precedence for the moment. He glanced over at her. Belinda had always been beautiful to him, but perhaps even more so today with her pink cheeks and joyful countenance. He flicked the reins and skirted the ranch before entering through a narrow canyon and back up a hill on the other side. For the next ten minutes, she attempted to solicit information from him as to where they were going. Several times over, he pretended to button his lip. He loved Belinda's curiosity, and while he had given in often in the past, he would resist this time.

He stared up and around to the gorgeous area overlooking the town of Hawthorne and the sprawling ranches beneath. The sun in the blue sky glistened off the snow, causing it to shimmer like diamonds. Ahead, a grove of numerous trees dotted the landscape. Otis pulled to one side and climbed from the sleigh. "Here we are." He offered a hand, and Belinda stood beside him.

"The view from here is amazing. I've never been up here before. How did you find this place?"

Otis wouldn't say that he'd nearly gotten himself lost, and that's how he had come upon the perfect place to find the perfect tree. Above them, western white pines with their bluish green needles formed an alcove. He inhaled deeply, never tiring of the scent that reminded him simultaneously of summer and Christmas. "Which one would you like?"

"For a Christmas tree?" A glint touched her eyes, and his heart stumbled in his chest.

"I thought we should have one in the house this year."

Her smile told him all he needed to know—that he'd made the right choice. She rushed toward him and wrapped her arms around his neck. "Thank you, Otis!"

He returned the hug. "I'm assuming you have decorations."

"Oh, yes, a whole attic full of them. I think Mara might be well enough tomorrow to help me collect some of them."

It took Belinda all of three minutes to decide on the perfect tree. A shorter, squattier one with perfectly splayed branches. Otis retrieved his ax from the sleigh and chopped it down.

When they returned to the Finnegan home, Otis hauled the tree into the house, and they set it up. Then he assisted Mara down the stairs. She marveled at the tree, and Otis chuckled, thinking of how much she reminded him of Anne-Marie.

He left the three women to decorate and ventured to town. There were three more things he needed to accomplish to make this a wonderful Christmas for

Belinda. First, he visited the post office, where the clerk informed him he had a telegram. His family was doing well and missed him. Wishing that Hawthorne had a telephone service like Hilltop did, Otis instead sent another telegram to his family saying Merry Christmas, that Mr. Finnegan's health had improved, and that Otis hoped to return home soon.

Otis then proceeded to stop at the mercantile. Hopefully, they would have just what he was looking for. The older woman, who, with her husband, owned the mercantile, assisted Otis with finding a harmonica.

"Do you play?" the woman asked.

"No, I don't, but I plan to learn within the next few hours." When the woman's jaw dropped, Otis figured he ought to elaborate. "Granted, I won't be hired to play in a band anytime soon, but I do hope to be able to provide some Christmas tunes." He removed the Chromatica harmonica made by the M Honor Company in Germany from its leather case. He blew a few notes on it and wished he could have covered his ears at the screeching that emitted from the instrument. Yes, he had much to accomplish before Christmas Day. While managing the chores at the Finnegan home, he could hopefully get a few practices in. He knew for certain that the cattle, horses, and chickens were a forgiving lot.

The woman then assisted him with a gift for Belinda. He had spent a significant amount of time musing over what to get her. He knew that she loved ornaments, and that while there was a box of them in the attic, he hoped few would be as precious as the ones he would purchase for her today. He lifted the decorated glass blue bulb, the flute-shaped red bulb, and the ten miniature round bulbs that reminded him of pearls on a necklace. "I'll take these as well."

The mercantile didn't have much food in stock yet, but it did have the other gifts for Belinda. He purchased a tin of Black Jack chewing gum and also a box of chocolates. The clerk graciously wrapped the items for him in brown paper. Since he was sleeping on the sofa at the Finnegan home, he had few places he could hide such things to keep them from being seen before Christmas. Perhaps he could tuck the gifts away in the barn.

Belinda needed to accomplish a few items in town before Christmas Eve. Since the stores were closed on Sunday, today was her only day. Ensuring that her family would be fine without her, Belinda first stopped at Leah's house. Just as they had in the past, they moseyed to the mercantile to pick out a gift for each of their family members.

She found the perfect gift for Otis—a top-quality knife with a silver-inlaid handle. She wished Hawthorne offered engraving options like the watchmaker shop in Hilltop.

But the most important gift she planned to give him could not be purchased. After she and Leah left the mercantile, Belinda proceeded to the post office. There, she asked the clerk if she could send a telegram to Hilltop. There was only a slim chance the recipients would receive it in time and be able to acquiesce, but it was worth the attempt.

On the way home, she had much to think about. While they were searching for a Christmas tree, she realized once again how much she loved Otis. For her, there would never be another. Had she lost her chance with him? Would he ever ask for her hand in courtship again? If she hadn't been so foolish, they would already be married by now.

She lifted her eyes to the brilliant blue sky and asked the Lord that if it was His will, Otis would give her a second chance. For the granting of such a request would be the perfect Christmas gift.

CHAPTER ELEVEN

BELINDA FOUND OTIS IN the barn that evening. There was so much she needed to say. So much she needed to resolve before more time passed. She would be remiss if she denied that she was quite nervous. Even though it was cold outside, she felt the sweat beads on the back of her neck. A nauseous feeling settled into her stomach, and her mouth was dry.

"Otis? Might we speak for a moment?"

Otis peered down at her from his place in the loft. Something about him seemed oddly suspicious. Was something amiss?

He swung one of his long legs over the edge and climbed down the ladder. "Uh...sure. Is everything all right?"

I hope it will be. How many times had she sought the Lord's guidance for this issue? "Yes, I just—I just needed to set things to rights."

His dark eyebrows rose to his forehead, and he regarded her.

Would she have the courage to discuss such a troublesome matter? Would he forgive her? He stood in front of her, and she again was reminded how dapper Otis MacCallum was. He was nearly a head taller than her, broad-shouldered, muscled, with long legs. But her favorite thing about him was his soft brown eyes. She realized she was staring, and heat swarmed up her neck and cheeks.

His mouth twitched into a smile. It relaxed her somewhat, and Belinda took a deep breath. "Otis, I owe you an apology." She stared down at her shoes before again lifting her gaze to his. When he said nothing, she continued. "I made one of the biggest mistakes in my life when—" her voice quivered. "When I declined your offer of courtship."

"It's all right, Belinda, you don't have to apologize."

She reached up and placed a finger on his lips. "Oh, but I do. I have looked back on that day with regret more times than I can count."

"If you didn't feel the same for me, you shouldn't be pressured into accepting my offer."

"But I did feel the same." Her heart splintered into a million little pieces as she thought of how he'd once felt for her. She'd been so blind.

Otis said nothing but cleared his throat. What was he thinking? Did he believe her?

"When you asked me that day, all I could think about was my parents moving to Hawthorne. We had just lost my grandparents within a week of each other, and my brother..."

"As I said, you don't have to apologize. I know you were struggling with some things that day, and I'm sorry for asking you when your mind was on all that you had been through."

"I honestly couldn't stop thinking of how my parents would have to move to my grandparents' home and start anew. We'd have to leave everything behind. All of the friends we'd made, our church, our ranch. You. While I didn't necessarily agree with Pa's choice to leave Hilltop, he felt it was the right thing to do."

Otis nodded. "I understand."

But Belinda wasn't sure he *did* understand. For how could he? Not fully, anyway. "When Pa and my brother had their disagreement, I thought it was like all of the other disagreements they'd had. They would later forgive each other and reconcile. But it wasn't the case this time." Her eyes misted. She would likely never hear from or see her brother again. But as hard as it was on her, she knew her parents grieved all the more. "Pa refused to give my brother the ranch in Hilltop because he needed to sell it in order to purchase more cattle here. My brother didn't understand. He wanted to continue ranching in Hilltop. That was our home. I know they spoke late into the night, although I wouldn't call it speaking as much as I would call it arguing."

"I'm so sorry, Belinda." Otis rested a hand on her arm.

Never could she have imagined that her brother would be estranged from the rest of the family over something such as land. Wasn't family more important than that? Where was the loyalty? What about a family having unconditional love for each other? What of Pa being unable to afford for them to reside in his own parents' home without the money from the Hilltop ranch?

"Thank you. Even as distraught as I was over my grandparents and my brother, I should not have treated you the way I did."

"I don't recall you being harsh."

She hadn't been harsh, but she had been the one to break his heart. "I just want to tell you I am sorry and that I regret that day more than I can express. Would you please forgive me?"

"I already have forgiven you."

The sincerity in his eyes said he spoke the truth, not that she would ever doubt his honesty. Otis was one of the most honest and forthright men she knew.

It was Christmas Eve Day, and Belinda hadn't much time to execute her final gift for Otis. She folded in the bread crumbs, molasses, a pinch of salt, suet, milk, raisins, citron, baking powder, and spices. She poured in the four well-beaten eggs and set them aside. The challenging part would be to allow the concoction to steam for four hours in a bucket.

Without Otis knowing.

She added to another bowl the creamed butter, an egg, and a cup of sugar. She stirred it into the boiling milk and tossed a dash of vanilla for flavor.

Belinda glanced out the window. From where she stood, she could see Otis tramping through the snow, minding the outside chores. If he came into the house, he would guess in an instant what she was baking. She tiptoed over to the window to get a better view of where he was headed. He had climbed on his horse and was riding toward the west pasture. She rushed back to the kitchen and commenced making the flaky pie crust in which to pour the plum pudding. Belinda inhaled the scrumptious scent, allowing it to settle into her lungs.

It smelled like Christmas.

Thoughts of Ma's cinnamon rolls entered her mind, but Belinda shoved the thought aside. It would give her something to look forward to next Christmas.

After she finished, Belinda allowed the mixture to cool sufficiently before setting it in the icebox. Thankfully, Otis was not the curious sort. Ma, Pa, and Mara were upstairs, so there was no threat of them catching a chill when Belinda flung the door open and allowed the crisp winter air to circulate through the room. Hopefully, by the time Otis returned for the noonday meal, the house would be completely cleared of any telltale scents.

Belinda plopped into the rocking chair and wrapped the blanket around her shoulders. She'd done it! Successfully made Otis's favorite Christmas dessert, and he was none the wiser. While she wished more than anything that he would have asked her again to court him, she was just grateful for the opportunity to seek his forgiveness—and even more so thankful when he offered that forgiveness.

Otis finished the chores as efficiently as he could. He hadn't much time if he wanted to achieve his final surprise for Belinda. He spurred his horse toward Glen's house. He suspected the man fancied Belinda, but right now, he needed Glen and his family's help to clinch his plan. When he arrived, he tethered his horse and knocked on Glen's parents' door. Ten minutes later, he was back on his horse and heading to the Finnegan ranch with a tin of cinnamon.

He was mucking out the stalls when Mrs. Finnegan entered the barn. He was grateful that both she and Mara had taken a turn for the better. The woman swiveled her head for a peek, likely to make sure Belinda hadn't followed her. "It's unfortunate we had to use all of the cinnamon while we were ill. Were you able to procure some more?"

Otis retrieved the spice from the saddlebag and handed it to her. "The question now will be how do we keep Belinda from knowing?"

Mrs. Finnegan again peered back at the door. "I have been wondering that this entire morning. Belinda is quite astute and might suspect if we aren't careful."

They discussed a few options before Mrs. Finnegan offered the perfect solution. "I do know Mara has been anxious to get outside the house after being confined for such a lengthy time. Why don't I suggest Belinda take Mara into town to see Leah and the baby? That would at least buy us some time for me to prepare the dough."

"I think that is a fantastic idea. I'll hitch the horse to the sleigh once she agrees."

Otis had never been one to hide what he was scheming. While he behaved himself as a young'un, Ma would be the first to say he'd been a bit mischievous a time or two. But she'd always determined his schemes. It still surprised him that Belinda couldn't tell that he still loved her just from his countenance.

Therefore, he would not be meandering near the sleigh after he hitched up the horse. Instead, he would check on the cattle. Because if Belinda saw his expression, she would know right away that he was plotting something.

After she left, Otis returned to the house. He stomped the snow off his boots, turned the doorknob, and entered the warmth of the Finnegan home. Mrs. Finnegan was busily preparing the bread dough and humming "What Child is This?" She turned when she heard him. "He's upstairs awake," she offered him a knowing smile, and Otis wondered how she figured out what he planned to do.

Otis removed his boots and walked up the stairs to Mr. and Mrs. Finnegan's room. Mr. Finnegan sat up in bed, reading one of the newspapers Doc had brought by during his rounds. The older man looked up from the paper. "Hello, Otis." His voice was still hoarse and nasally, but Otis thanked the Lord he was much improved.

"Good afternoon, sir."

"I've been looking at an advertisement for Christmas gifts. Unfortunately, with being busy and all, I haven't had the opportunity to go Christmas shopping." A smirk appeared on Mr. Finnegan's weary and pale face, and Otis chuckled. "Do you think when I am able to go back to the mercantile again, that the missus would appreciate a pair of fur-trimmed slippers?"

Otis knew nothing about slippers and even less about women's slippers. Purchasing Belinda the ornaments had been much easier. He shrugged. "She probably would."

Mr. Finnegan offered a weak laugh. "Mara and I were up here writing out coupons with the gifts my family will receive after Christmas."

"Excellent idea."

Belinda's father nodded. "I thought so. I want to thank you, Otis, for staying here at the ranch and helping. I'm not sure what we would have done without you."

"Happy to do so. I'm grateful you're feeling much better."

"As am I. God sure answered some prayers." Mr. Finnegan took a drink of the water on the table beside his bed. "I reckon you're up here checking on my health, but something tells me there's more."

Otis had known the Finnegans for a good long time, and so it was no surprise that Mr. Finnegan suspected something might be amiss. "Yes, sir, I do have a question for you." Why did Otis's muscles feel so twitchy? He tugged on the outside of his collar. Mr. Finnegan was like a second father. Why the intense nerves?

The man set the paper by his side and gave Otis his full attention. "What can I help you with, son?"

"As you may or may not know, I am fond of Belinda."

"I suspected as much. I also knew that she declined

your offer before we moved."

"She did."

Mr. Finnegan stroked his unkempt beard. "Always wondered what happened between you two. Belinda never said. Or at least to me, anyhow."

"Yes, sir, it was a disappointment. However, I believe we've worked things out now."

"That's good to hear. Always appreciate it when two folks reconcile, especially when it's you and Belinda. Always did figure you two would end up married someday."

The sweat beaded on Otis's forehead. Mr. Finnegan had figured that, even after what had happened? He cleared his throat and shoved his hands in his pants pockets. "I'd like to ask her to be my wife." Even as Otis said the words aloud, a slip of fear wormed its way through him. What if she said no again?

"You have my blessing. The missus and I couldn't ask for a better man to marry our daughter or a better man to have as a son-in-law. Do you plan to ask for her hand in courtship first?"

"I think I will just ask her to marry me, but I do know that if she says yes, we will court for as long as she would like. I know I'll be taking her from her family, which would be an adjustment."

"According to the paper here, they're talking of building a railroad spur between Hilltop and Hawthorne. Once that's complete, it won't be so far at all. Besides, it's time the Finnegan family paid a few visits to Hilltop. We miss our friends there."

"Yes, sir," Otis wiped his sweaty palms on his pants.

"Thank you, sir, for giving me your blessing. I promise if she says yes, I'll be a good and faithful husband."

"I have no doubt. And I also do not doubt that she will be amenable to your proposal."

Otis, more than anything else, hoped Mr. Finnegan was correct.

CHAPTER TWELVE

BELINDA SUSPECTED THAT SOMETHING was afoot. Ma had practically pushed her and Mara out the door, and when they arrived at the sleigh conveniently hitched to the horse and ready to go, Otis was nowhere to be found. She smiled to herself. Christmas was full of surprises, and knowing Otis, she had no doubt he may have planned one or two of his own.

Their first stop when entering Hawthorne was to see if there was a return telegram for her. Unfortunately, there wasn't. Next, she and Mara visited with Leah and the baby. They enjoyed cups of hot chocolate while engaging in pleasant conversation before beginning a family tradition of crafting a wreath for the front door. It didn't matter how often Belinda and Leah spoke—they always found more things to talk about.

When they had a modicum of privacy, Leah leaned toward her and whispered, "How are things going between you and Otis?"

Belinda tossed a glance at her younger sister, who was immersed in playing patty-cake with Baby Ethel. "I was able to apologize, and he has forgiven me."

"I'm not surprised that he would forgive you. Otis is a very gracious man. That's why I'm still bamboozled at the thought that you didn't accept his proposal last spring."

Leah knew more than anyone else about the situation with Otis. "What I wish is that he would ask me again."

"And if he did, would you say yes this time?"

"I most certainly would without hesitation."

"How are things coming along with the surprises?"

"Quite well. There's only one I'm not sure about, but I am hopeful. The main thing, of course, is celebrating Jesus' birth, and I'm grateful for so many things this Christmas. Namely, that we are all either completely better or in the process of healing. I was worried about losing Pa."

"I was as well." Leah pulled Belinda into a side hug. They spent more time together before Belinda and Mara bid Leah and Ethel goodbye, and they returned to the ranch, wreath in hand. Belinda wasn't sure she could sleep tonight with the excitement of all the upcoming festivities.

Otis doubted he would be able to catch any shut-eye tonight, what with his anticipation for tomorrow. He'd been unable to focus his attention on chores. His mind was in a dither, and his stomach in knots. *Lord, please let me ask her in Your perfect timing.*

He gathered the eggs from the chickens and stepped back out into the frosty day. Cow barked, and Otis looked up to see Belinda rounding the corner toward the house as if a skilled sleigh driver. That was another thing he loved about Belinda. She was capable. But would she be willing to leave her home behind? He thought of the house he had worked steadfastly to build for their future. Would she like it? He hoped she would add her own decorating as he wanted it to be their home together rather than just his. Otis only wished he had brought the ring from Hilltop, but who knew when he left that day how things would transpire?

"What do you think, Cow? Do you think Belinda will say yes when I ask her tomorrow?"

Cow bobbed her head as though she understood, and maybe she did. His dog was fond of Belinda as well, although she had spent an inordinate amount of time snuggling Mara during their visit to Hawthorne.

After all the presents were opened tomorrow, he hoped to take Belinda aside and ask her the question that had been on his heart and mind for some time.

He followed Cow into the house. Earlier today, he had scanned the area from one of the corrals and noticed the door was open. He'd been about to check on the matter when someone shut it. The observation puzzled him as the weather was far too cold for the door to remain ajar for long. He delivered the eggs into the house, then loaded up several armloads of firewood and delivered them beside the fireplace. He wanted everyone to be warm and cozy for the Christmas festivities tomorrow.

That evening, after hanging the wreath Belinda had made, he placed the gifts beneath the tree. He hoped Belinda wouldn't browse through the presents because she would likely guess the chewing gum with its flavorful licorice-scented aroma.

He would miss the traditions his own family started years ago. Would they wait to open the gifts he'd purchased for them until he returned? Either way, he was thankful he'd been able to help the Finnegan family in their time of need.

Belinda could hardly sit still. Would the MacCallums be arriving? As of yesterday, she hadn't received a return telegram. She set the turkey in the oven and cast a glance at Otis, who sat talking with Pa and Tom, Cow perched in his lap. Things were mended between them, and she appreciated his forgiveness. Would he someday ask again for her hand in marriage? If he did, she would certainly say yes without hesitation. Never again would she make the same error. She loved him. Wanted to spend the rest of her life with him.

Yes, it would be a change to leave her family behind in Hawthorne. They'd always been close, and she would want to visit them often.

His gaze met hers, and she quickly averted her attention to the stack of plates on the table. Leah nudged her. "I saw that," she whispered.

"Saw what?" Heat warmed Belinda's cheeks.

"I'm thrilled you two have reconciled."

"Me, too." Belinda bit her lip and again peered at Otis.

Such a godly, kind, and dapper man. What would she have done if he hadn't been there to assist them? To bring supplies to Hawthorne? To come alongside her family in their time of need? She scanned the room. It was only by God's grace that her family was recovering. Ma was doing much better, and Mara, while she was still weak, continued to improve. Every day, Pa grew stronger. Doc assured them it would take some time, but that Pa was certainly on the mend. Things could have transpired so differently.

Mara, with the help of Ethel, distributed the presents. Would Otis cotton to the new pocket knife? She'd purposely set the plum pudding pie upstairs in her room so he wouldn't discover it. Would it taste as delicious as Mrs. Stroud's?

Otis removed the brown paper. "Thank you, Belinda." The way his eye caught hers caused her stomach to flutter.

"You're welcome. We have one other thing for you." She bolted upstairs to retrieve the plum pudding pie. The golden edges and the mixture sandwiched between the top and bottom crusts looked almost as delicious as the colored illustration in Ma's cookbook, if she did say so herself.

Please, Lord, let it taste delectable. She offered the prayer, then carefully lifted the confection from its place on the dresser. "Otis, close your eyes and hold out your hands," she announced from the top of the stairs. She carefully descended the steps and placed the pie in his splayed hands. "You can open them."

"Is this plum pudding pie?"

"It is."

Otis's brown eyes enlarged, and he licked his lips. "Reckon I won't be waiting until supper for a taste test."

Mara giggled. "It's Christmas, Otis. You can eat dessert first."

Belinda handed him a spoon, and Otis scooped a generous piece of pie from the tin and shoveled it into his mouth. She held her breath, awaiting his response.

He finished chewing and nodded. "It's delicious, Belinda, thank you."

"Are you fixing to share?" asked Tom.

Otis jokingly pulled it closer to his red flannel shirt. "I'm a generous man in most cases, but when it comes to plum pudding pie..."

A round of chuckles ensued, and Belinda released the breath she'd been holding.

"Now it's your turn to close your eyes and hold out your hands," instructed Ma.

Belinda did as requested, and she heard shuffling before something akin to a pan was placed in her outstretched hands. "You can open your eyes," said Otis.

She did so and marveled at the cinnamon rolls. "Did you bake these, Otis?"

He chuckled that pleasing, rumbling laugh she'd grown to love. "No, your ma did."

"However, it was Otis's idea since we couldn't very well avoid tradition."

"I had no idea that with the illnesses and all—" Belinda's voice caught. "Thank you, Ma. Thank you, Otis."

They continued opening presents. Otis handed her a square box, and Belinda methodically removed the lovely wrap. "They're beautiful," she gasped. She lifted a flute-shaped red bulb and held it to her heart. "I love these. Thank you." How had he known such a gift would be so meaningful?

"Two more gifts."

"Two?"

He nodded, that crooked smile she'd loved all these years lighting his face. He deposited two tins into her hands.

"Chewing gum! Thank you, Otis—this is my favorite kind." She held the Black Jack chewing gum to her nose and inhaled. "And chocolates!" her mouth watered.

There was something so very special about someone who knew so much about you. Your likes, dislikes, and even your favorite type of gum. A sharp pain stabbed through her heart at the thought that she could have missed entirely the one God had planned for her.

They were opening presents when a loud knock erupted on the door. Cow barked and wagged her tail.

"Who could that be?" Mr. Finnegan asked.

Otis watched as Belinda and her mother exchanged a glance. He thought he might have seen Mrs. Finnegan wink. Mara hobbled to the door and opened it.

"Merry Christmas!"

Otis stood and gazed out the doorway. He closed his eyes, opened them again, squinted, then widened them.

Could it be? Was he dreaming? He hadn't slept as well as he'd hoped last night. Perhaps he was overly tired.

Two seconds passed, and he realized that his family truly was in Hawthorne, and not only in Hawthorne, but at the Finnegan home.

Pa limped in with two crutches and stopped to pat Otis on the back. "Good to see you, son."

Mart jabbed him in the ribs and smirked. "Where have you been?"

Anne-Marie toddled in and gave Otis a cursory glance and nod of her head before scooping Cow up into her arms.

Ma reached up and framed his face with her hands. "We've missed you so much, sweet boy."

Grandma wrapped him in a warm hug before taking a step back. "You look like you've grown since I last saw you." She pinched his cheek, then pivoted her gaze toward the sleigh just as Otis heard Grandpa's voice.

"Could someone help me out?"

Grandma laughed and patted Otis on the arm. "We had to make sure he stayed nice and warm after having been so sick, but would you be a dear and assist your grandfather out of the sleigh?"

Otis's heart felt light. This was the best Christmas present he could ask for, and he figured he knew just who was behind the surprise. He yanked on his boots and then sauntered out to the sleigh. Grandpa was in the back, surrounded by numerous quilts. "It's about time someone came to rescue me." Because blankets devoured him, Grandpa's fuzzy eyebrows and red nose were the only things one could see.

Minutes later, the MacCallum and Finnegan families crowded around the table and sofa, just like old times in Hilltop. Otis withdrew his harmonica from his pocket.

"I never knew you owned a harmonica," said Mart.

"I just purchased it and have been practicing in the barn for Cow, the horses, and the chickens. I know how much Belinda appreciates harmonica songs."

Ma smiled. "Otis, you have always been one who could learn anything you set your mind to."

Otis nodded toward Mr. Finnegan. "Are you feeling well enough to play a few songs?"

"Not sure I'll be able to get my lungs to cooperate, but I'm impressed that you've learned to play in such a short amount of time."

"Otis playing the harmonica?" Mart shook his head. "Poor Cow." He scratched behind Cow's ears. "How did you survive? Was it any better than Otis's singing?"

Otis glowered at his younger brother. "Says the one who invites a wide berth around him while singing at church."

"Or when we went Christmas caroling last year." Anne-Marie shuddered. "As I recall, Mart was in the front row all alone. Trust us, Otis. You're a much better singer than Mart."

That caused a round of laughter, and Mart offered an exaggerated bow.

"I, for one, would love to hear Otis play the harmonica." Grandma Etta Mae leaned over and patted Otis on the arm. "What will you play for us, dear?"

It had seemed like such a simple thing to do for Belinda when the thought first pricked his mind, but now, in front of everyone with his unskilled inexperience, he was having second thoughts. His original plan was to play Belinda's favorite song, "Away in a Manger", then hand the instrument to Mr. Finnegan, who could play "God Rest Ye Merry, Gentlemen", as Mr. Finnegan had every year when the MacCallums and Finnegans joined for Christmas.

Was it too late to change his mind?

"I, uh…"

All eyes were on him, but there was really only one pair of eyes that mattered. He caught a look of admiration in Belinda's gaze. They'd sung a song or two on their buggy rides and lifted their voices in chorus during church worship. Would he be able to play a suitable tune with the harmonica? A case of the nerves attacked him, and a droplet of sweat trickled down his back. It helped that Ma had ensured her children took piano lessons, but a piano wasn't a harmonica. He would put forth his best effort, but Otis was not a musician.

"I would love to hear you play the harmonica." The sweet tinkle of Belinda's encouragement interrupted Otis's apprehension. He squared his shoulders, rubbed a finger across the Chromatica, then lifted it to his lips. If Belinda had faith he wouldn't sound like a squeaky hinge, he could uphold his promise.

Otis folded his hands over the instrument and blew the first few notes. His trepidation waned, and even in his own ears, it didn't sound too dreadful.

Belinda lifted her voice to harmonize with the music, and several of the others joined her, along with Cow, who offered her own rendition.

His makeshift crowd clapped. "That wasn't half bad," quipped Mart. "Maybe you ought to ask Pastor Gunderson if you can play for the congregation."

"That would be delightful. Mrs. Jowett has wanted to assemble a church choir for some time. She could play the piano, Otis could play the harmonica, and those who'd like to sing may do so." Grandma Etta Mae peered from person to person, likely in hopes someone would agree.

Otis wouldn't be one of those. "I appreciate the sentiment, Grandma, but I'd prefer to stay in the pew with my hymnal."

After Otis played "God Rest Ye Merry, Gentlemen" because Mr. Finnegan was unable to do so, Pa read the Christmas story from the Book of Luke. They ate supper, then Otis joined the menfolk and discussed the recent elections and President Roosevelt's trips to Puerto Rico and Panama. But his mind was never far from Belinda. He hoped to ask her that all-important question before the day was over.

Baby Ethel took to attempting to ride Cow. Of course, Cow, with her easygoing and agreeable personality, complied.

"It wasn't that long ago that Otis was riding Cow," Ma said.

Everyone laughed, and Otis groaned. This wasn't the first time the story had been told.

"He loved the former Cow," added Pa.

At her name being spoken, Cow wandered over to Otis, Ethel on her back, and nuzzled Otis's arm. "Don't worry, Cow. I love you too."

She barked, and Ethel giggled.

Otis focused his attention on Belinda as he watched her from across the room. She'd thrown her head back, cheerfully laughing at something Leah said. His heart beat more steadily in his chest. She caught his gaze, and their eyes connected. Would now be a good time to ask the question on his mind? He'd prayed about it all day. Would she say yes? Otis stood and walked to where Belinda sat on the sofa with Ma, Leah, and Mrs. Finnegan. Anne-Marie and Mara sat on chairs adjacent to the sofa, their giggles rising above the other multiple conversations.

Anne-Marie smirked at him. She was far too nosy for her own good. He ignored her and the curious glances from Ma and Mrs. Finnegan. If he let this day get away, he'd never muster up the nerve again. Or at least not while he remained in Hawthorne. He and his family would leave tomorrow. When would he see her again? Or maybe he should wait until tomorrow. Otis wrung his hands. He wasn't normally a nervous man. But so much was at stake this time. Especially his heart.

He doubted it could take rejection twice over.

"Whatcha doing, Otis?" Anne-Marie jabbed Mara in the side and nodded toward Belinda.

"You look suspicious, Otis," added Mara.

"How come you're not talking with the menfolk? Prefer to chat about quilts and the latest news from Hilltop?" Anne-Marie tapped her chin. "Or, maybe you wish to speak with a certain someone?"

Perhaps later would be a better time. Later, when Anne-Marie and Mara found something else to do with themselves besides tormenting him with their questions and prattling on like featherbrained hens.

"Is that certain someone Belinda?" asked Mara.

A rosy blush covered Belinda's face. She looked lovely in her white shirtwaist and the red skirt Ma had made. It accentuated her figure, and her countenance glowed. For a minute, Otis forgot all about why he was standing there.

"Belinda?"

"Yes?"

Suddenly, the entire room grew quiet.

"Could I speak with you?"

"You most certainly can speak with her," offered Anne-Marie.

He narrowed his eyes at his vexatious sister. Someday, if she ever had a suitor, Otis would be sure to return the favor.

"Yes." Belinda stood, and Otis offered her his elbow.

"Reckon we could get some fresh air on the porch."

"I'll fetch my coat."

Mara's hoarse voice rose a few decibels. "Ooh, they're going to the porch."

That elicited all kinds of commentary from the womenfolk and some comment from Mart that Otis couldn't quite discern.

He tossed on his own coat and opened the door for Belinda. He followed her to the porch and was about to express the words on his heart when he turned and noticed two faces squished against the glass of the front window.

Two familiar faces.

Two faces that belonged to two exasperating girls.

Was there nowhere to obtain privacy on this crisp Christmas evening?

"I was hoping to talk with you about something," he said. He led Belinda to the far edge of the porch away from prying eyes. His original intent was to get down on one knee, but he didn't have the ring.

The door opened a crack.

"Anne-Marie, Mara, we see you."

"Oh, crumbles. He saw us," muttered Anne-Marie. She hesitantly closed the door, and finally, Otis and Belinda were alone.

Otis gulped a steadying breath, sent a desperate prayer heavenward, then summoned the courage. "Belinda Finnegan, I love you. Will you marry me?"

"Yes."

"Yes?"

"Yes."

"Because I know you might not be sure about it, and I know..."

She reached up and pressed a delicate finger to his lips. "Yes, Otis MacCallum, I will marry you. I would be honored to be your wife."

He lifted her into his arms, their faces mere inches apart. "Might I offer a Christmas kiss to finalize it?"

"I'd be particularly fond of a Christmas kiss."

Their eyes locked, and she parted her lips to meet his kiss.

EPILOGUE

DECEMBER 21, 1907

THE WEDDING DRESS MRS. MacCallum sewed for this special occasion was more elegant and lovely than Belinda could have ever imagined. Elaborate beading on the bodice, waistband, and trimming the bottom edge of the dress, along with a lace neckline, assured it was the most exquisite dress in all of Montana, if not the entire country.

Tears shimmered in Ma's eyes. "You look beautiful."

Leah tucked a wayward strand of Belinda's hair into the stylish and wavy Gibson girl coiffure she'd decorated with a matching flowers-and-pearl hairpin.

"I've never seen a lovelier bride," added Grandma Etta Mae. "And to think when you and Otis have children, Vann and I will be great-great-grandparents." She held a wrinkled hand to her bosom. "Goodness, me."

Heat flamed Belinda's cheeks. Oh, yes, she and Otis had discussed having a family.

A knock at the door sounded. "Not to interrupt, but lest the bride be late, figure you should all be boarding the sleigh by now."

"We're coming, Vann," assured Grandma Etta Mae.

"Thank you, Mrs. MacCallum, for the dress."

"You are more than welcome." The woman took both of Belinda's hands in her own. "There's no one else I'd rather have for a daughter-in-law."

"Even if it took you far longer than necessary to realize you two were meant for each other," quipped Grandma Etta Mae.

Grandpa Vann delivered the sleigh to the front door, and Ma, Mrs. MacCallum, and Grandma Etta Mae assisted Belinda into the sleigh. Mara and Anne-Marie hoisted themselves into the back of the sleigh, all the while giggling and carrying on. Leah and Ethel squeezed in. "Cow go with us, Mama?" Ethel pointed a finger at the porch where Cow and Boots sat, their tails wagging.

"No, sweetie, not this time."

Grandma Etta Mae took the reins and beckoned the horses, and the sleigh glided across the newly fallen snow. The sun shone brightly, and the pine trees that lined the drive tipped their snow-covered branches.

"Oh, dear. There's Otis!" Grandma Etta Mae swerved the sleigh to the side of the road as Ma and Mrs. MacCallum simultaneously held up a blanket to shield Belinda from Otis's sight.

Grandma Etta Mae shook her head, her gray bun bobbing as she did so. "What's he doing out here? We can't have the groom seeing the bride."

"He turned the other way," reassured Mara.

The groom. The bride. In less than an hour, Belinda would be a married woman. Married to the man she'd loved for longer than she realized.

When they reached the church, Belinda was ushered

into the parsonage while the final preparations were made. The entire town was in attendance, along with some who'd traveled from Hawthorne. Folks crowded along the edges of the church, and Mrs. Jowett had donated some of her silk flowers for the edges of the pews and for Mara, Ethel, and Anne-Marie—Belinda's flower girls—and Leah, her matron of honor, to carry.

Pa walked Belinda to the front of the church. She thought she saw an unshed tear in his eye. Thankfully, he'd fully recovered and was back to his former self. Was it just a year ago that Belinda feared they would lose him?

Otis awaited her, so dapper in his black suit that emphasized his broad shoulders. His soft-brown eyes shone.

Pastor Gunderson recited the vows, pronounced them man and wife, then informed Otis he may kiss his bride. The velvet warmth of his kiss sealed their vows, and Belinda's heart pattered double-time in her chest. Ah, but to live every day for the rest of her life with this man God had saved just for her.

And to think she'd almost missed her chance.

This would most assuredly be a Christmas to remember.

Love *in* DISGUISE

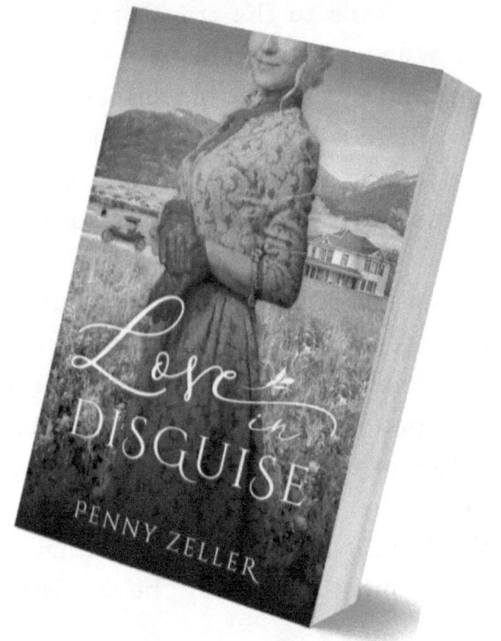

WHO KNEW CONCEALING ONE'S TRUE
IDENTITY COULD BE SO DISASTROUS?

Love in Disguise
Preview

"THOSE COWS ARE GOING to drive me plumb out of my mind," Emilie Crawford Wheeler muttered. She stood on her porch, hands on her hips, glaring at the herd of Black Angus cows taking a tour of her front yard.

Heart pounding, she reached for the porch pillar for support. Just because she had inherited the ranch from her late husband didn't mean she particularly cared for the abhorrent creatures.

Their boisterous mooing echoed throughout the otherwise quiet Montana afternoon. Emilie watched as they trampled through her yard, destroying or eating every piece of vegetation in their path.

Her beautiful oak tree sapling, which had withstood storms and hail, became the most recent casualty, its tender limbs snapping beneath a particularly large cow's hoof.

One cow swaggered up the porch steps as if such a feat were an ordinary, everyday spectacle. "Shoo!" she yelled while removing her hat and flapping it about. The cow paid her no mind but continued to occupy the far end of the porch.

While concentrating on the cow on the porch, Emilie didn't realize until too late that a Black Angus had leaned its head over the railing and commenced chewing on her hat, slowly and methodically, as if it were part of its normal diet. "Well, I never!" she exclaimed.

She best act quickly if she was to halt the destruction of her newly-planted gardens.

Emilie turned on her heel and ran into the house, ignoring the startled looks from her staff. Instead, she reached into the closet and retrieved Newt's shotgun.

"Almira, dear, please do remember proper etiquette and that you must always conduct yourself as a lady." Mother's admonishment using Emilie's given name threatened to stop her from her course of action.

But she must forge ahead on her mission to finally rectify the problem with the neighbor's cows. And why was it the man was never home when she wished to discuss the situation? Did Mr. Evanson even exist? Or did the ranch running parallel to hers operate itself?

Whoever coined the phrase that desperate times called for desperate measures must have dealt with rogue cattle and their propensity to destroy everything in their path.

"Almira, ladies do not fire weapons. Please do reconsider." What Mother might say were she in Hollow Creek thrummed through Emilie's mind.

"Mother, this is an emergency," she said aloud, nearly stomping through the house.

There was no time for proper etiquette. Today Annie Oakley would be her hero. Miss Oakley was a lady, after all, and Emilie thought of just how accurately she might mimic the woman's skill with a gun.

"Is everything all right, Mrs. Wheeler?" Hattie asked, concern lining the maid's youthful features.

"Quite all right, Hattie, thank you for asking."

"Is it the cows again?"

"Yes, it is, and I have every mind to…"

"Will Cook be preparing steak for supper, Emilie?" Vera, her housekeeper, asked as she entered the room, a smirk on her sweet wrinkled face.

Emilie smiled, thankful for the humorous reprieve from the current situation.

Vera placed a hand on Emilie's arm. "Let us help you," she offered. "Morris has gone to town, but surely you, Hattie, and I can do something to deter the cattle until the hands come to rectify the situation. We might be able to save some of your yard."

"Well, someone has to do something about Mr. Evanson's cows." That someone would be her. While it was never admirable to be prone to temper, and Emilie did not consider herself a temperamental woman, she had all she could take with that ninnyhammer Mr. Evanson and his assemblage of bovine.

This was not the first time they demolished her yard, but it would be the last.

"*Almira, do contain yourself,*" Mother would say.

But there was no containing in this matter. Emilie flung open the door and stalked out onto her porch. A few chickens had escaped from the coop and joined the circus in her front yard, squawking and doing their best to avoid being trampled. Emilie checked to be sure no one was in danger of her Annie Oakley ways, then, walking from beneath the porch roof, raised the shotgun to the air and fired a shot.

Several of the cows turned and ran from the yard, but a few stayed staring at her. "Shoo! I said shoo!" Emilie shouted to the remaining cattle.

The cows kicked up dust and continued encroaching upon her property, causing a most appalling commotion.

Jep, one of her hired hands, rounded the corner then, his scrawny torso barely keeping up with his long legs. "We have this all taken care of, Mrs. Wheeler. No need to worry yourself none."

It looked far from taken care of, but Emilie didn't mention such. Two of her other ranch hands appeared on horseback and attempted to herd the cattle back to Mr. Evanson's pasture.

Emilie set the shotgun against the house and patted her skirts, releasing puffs of dust. She was going to faint dead away if she did not get a reprieve from those dastardly cows and their even more dastardly owner.

Vera joined her on the porch. "A trip to Missoula is just the thing you need. Besides, you could deliver those gifts to the orphanage on your way there and see the children."

"What a splendid idea. I shall leave tomorrow morning. However, I think I may just retrieve more presents for the children while in Missoula, and stop there on the way back."

"Excellent plan! Children can never have too many presents. Do you wish for Morris and me to accompany you?"

Emilie thought for a moment, gazing at the seemingly futile effort of Jep and her other hired hands to contain the raucous cattle. "While I do so enjoy the company of you and Morris, I believe I shall make this journey to Missoula on my own."

"Some time away will be of benefit."

Some time away was just what Emilie needed. Being proper-like with a dash of rebellion wasn't for the faint of heart.

Early the following morning, Emilie packed her bags for her trip to Missoula. She needed to retrieve the brand-new hat she'd ordered from Miss Julia Mathilda's Fine Dresses. And not a moment too soon since she was now one hat less due to that cow's insidious appetite. Besides, a break would do her good and shopping did seem to fix many a problem.

Jep carried several wrapped gifts to her Model T to donate to the orphanage. If there was a charity close to her heart, the orphanage would garner that distinction. Each month, she donated a generous check to the institution, as well as a variety of items she purchased in Missoula on her many outings to the city.

Because of the weather and the urgency to return home, she had been unable to stop at the orphanage during her most recent trip. It would be good to stop by, see the children, and gift them with the special books, clothes, and toys she previously purchased for them.

Yes, perhaps a trip to Missoula and the orphanage would improve her mood after having her entire front yard destroyed. At least the west side gardens were unscathed.

Huge miracle that was.

Morris started the Model T, opened the door for Emilie to board, and within five minutes, she tasted the freedom of the open road.

Nearly two hours later, she came to a stop at the carriage house behind Missoula's Bellerose Hotel and Restaurant. A fine supper, followed by a restful night's sleep in the feather bed in room twenty-three, the room where she always stayed during her visits, would refresh her mind.

And tomorrow?

Tomorrow the promise of shopping awaited her. For surely shopping would rid her mind completely of despicable cows and contemptible neighbors.

All would be well.

Oh, why, oh why, had she not chosen to employ the delivery service? No wonder the clerk at Miss Julia Mathilda's Fine Dresses looked askance when she had declined.

Nevertheless, she straightened her posture and attempted to toss aside the twinge of regret. Determination forced her toward her destination and precluded her from turning around and retracing her wobbly steps to Miss Mathilda's.

Emilie stumbled down the boardwalk toward the Bellerose Hotel and Restaurant as she peeked from one side of the tall tower of parcels to the other. They teetered precariously, and with much effort, Emilie righted them. Several folks sauntered past her, most of whom were careful to watch for the woman wearing the oversized wide-brimmed hat with the six boxes and three bags situated in and on her arms.

Where was the Bellerose Hotel and Restaurant? Shouldn't she have reached it by now?

Emilie's right arm had fallen asleep, and her left ached from its awkward position toting the heavy load. Such stubbornness on her part, this endeavor to carry her own parcels.

But was not such an endeavor a necessary part of her newfound freedom? A freedom Emilie had never before experienced? A freedom she planned to embrace?

Pride might be an appropriate term, not that Emilie would admit it.

Mother's choice word for the situation would be *impudent.* She would be shaking her head and her perfectly coifed curls with dismay at her daughter's choice. Her voice would take on a disapproving tone. *"Almira Emilie Crawford Wheeler,"* she would say, her hands on hips.

Emilie teetered from one foot to the other, desperately trying to balance on the high heels of her fashionable button-up leather boots. The stack of parcels leaned to the left, then to the right. The three bags situated on her arms slid down to her wrists, causing an off-balanced jolt into the stacked parcels.

She was on the verge of recovering from her precarious situation when the most devastating event occurred.

Someone bumped into her right shoulder. It wasn't that it was a hard bump, or even a rowdy bump, but it did totter her nearly plumb off her feet and toward the left.

And her parcel with the new hat? It plummeted to the ground and tumbled into the street. Flinging the rest of her purchases haphazardly to the side, Emilie darted toward the parcel as it rolled into the path of an oncoming wagon. Desperate to save her hat, Emilie absentmindedly stumbled into the path of traffic.

Just as she reached for the prized possession, a strong hand clasped her upper arm and pulled her back onto the boardwalk. Emilie batted at the firm grip, her focus remaining on the parcel.

Her breath squeezed from her lungs, as she watched a horse trample the hatbox and its precious contents.

No. No. No!

Stunned, Emilie wrenched herself free from the grasp and staggered in shock to retrieve the crushed box. *Surely the hat will be fine. The box is made of only the finest materials.*

She stumbled back to the boardwalk. Holding her breath, she lifted the mangled lid and gaped in horror.

Her precarious situation momentarily forgotten, she winced at the condition of her once-lavish hat. The tattered and formerly ornate ostrich feather floated wistfully to the ground, a sure sign her poor hat had not survived the cruel fate it was handed. Never again would the crushed accessory be wearable.

It had been a splendid hat of 1911 fashion that had boasted a marvelous ostrich feather. Ordered from one of the most renowned millineries in Boston, it emanated elegance and high-class fashion. Now it was ruined.

What was left of it, anyway.

Whatever was she to do? Emilie had intended the new hat to replace the one she wore at present, as the former was becoming far too 1910. While she didn't have too terribly many material weaknesses, she did appreciate the latest fashions.

As if losing a hat to a cow yesterday wasn't bad enough, now she must lose one to a horse.

Could things get any worse? As Emilie lamented her situation, a most ghastly incident occurred. Her toe caught the edge of one of the parcels she had tossed aside, and she lost her footing and tumbled to the ground. She landed in an unladylike heap on the boardwalk.

She closed her eyes for a moment, willing that no one witnessed her unfortunate lack of respectability. *So much for propriety and decorum.*

Then she remembered all of her parcels, especially the once-elegant hat, strewn all about her. Trying not to appear as inept as she felt, Emilie contemplated how best to retrieve those parcels.

And restore her dignity.

A disturbing thought entered her mind: how would she lift the parcels off the ground and re-stack them in her arms?

An even more disturbing thought then clouded her mind. Would she ever regain her composure?

"Ma'am?"

Emilie gazed up into the bluest of blue eyes she had ever seen. Her eyes locked with his, and she sucked in her breath. Suddenly her parcels and her ill-fated hat were forgotten. She squinted at him. His mouth was moving, but in her discombobulated state, she could neither focus on nor hear a word.

In all of her etiquette lessons, never had there been instructions on how to behave properly when sprawled in a most unrefined manner in the middle of the boardwalk in front of a handsome stranger.

Whatever would Mother say now?

If you want to be among the first to hear about Penny's latest book projects, sign up for her newsletter at her website at www.pennyzeller.com. You will receive book and writing updates, encouragement, notification of current giveaways, occasional freebies, and special offers.

If you enjoyed this glimpse into the lives of Belinda
and Otis, please consider leaving a review on your
social media, Amazon, Goodreads, Barnes and Noble, or
BookBub. Reviews are critical to authors, and those stars
you give us are such an encouragement.

Author's Note

Dear Reader,

Thank you for spending some time in Montana with me for Otis and Belinda's story. Initially, I planned for *Heart of Courage* to be a standalone book; however, readers reached out to me asking for a story about Otis as an adult. After much prayer, his story became a reality.

Otis, of course, needed a love interest, and who better than Belinda, who had rejected his marriage proposal? These two characters became real to me, and I found as I was writing the book that I, myself, was rooting for them.

A Christmas to Remember was an enjoyable story to write. I, too, was excited to see how LilyBeth, Barrett, Otis, Etta Mae, and Vann were doing after all these years. While it can be read as a standalone, I wanted to be sure to include some connections to *Heart of Courage*, especially pertaining to Cow. As in all of my books, there is plentiful humor, but this book also included some sad moments as well with so many suffering from influenza and pneumonia, then sometimes referred to as lung fever.

I spent a lot of time researching illnesses and medicinal and natural cures. Opiates were often used in this time period for a variety of ailments. Dover's Powder and Chamberlain's Cough Remedy were real. In December of 1906, the Petrified Forest Monument was created by President Theodore Roosevelt. Barrett's Oldsmobile was delivered from Michigan, as were many automobiles in that day. An Oldsmobile climbing Mount Snowdon in Great Britain is also factual.

Something interesting I discovered while writing *A Christmas to Remember* was that plum pudding pie does not have plums in the recipe, or rather, it didn't in the original recipe. It does, however, have bread crumbs, molasses, suet, milk, raisins, citron, spices, and more. Some plum pudding pie recipes did include alcohol. The plum pudding pie for this book was the alcohol-free version.

One of the things that made this book special was the closeness of the family members. When things were tough, everyone pitched in and helped each other.

As always, thank you for your continued loyalty in reading my books. Thank you for spending time within the pages of this book for Otis and Belinda's story. Until next time, happy reading!

Blessings,

Penny

ACKNOWLEDGMENTS

To my family who continually walk with me through this crazy writing gig. I couldn't do it without you!

To my Penny's Peeps Street Team. Thank you for spreading the word about my books, for always being so willing to read and review my stories, and for your steadfast encouragement and support.

To my beta readers. You are the ones who see my project at its beginning stages. Thank you for all of your wonderful suggestions.

To my readers, may God bless you and guide you as you grow in your walk with Him.

And, most importantly, thank you to my Lord and Savior, Jesus Christ. It is my deepest desire to glorify You with my writing and help bring others to a knowledge of Your saving grace.

About the Author

Penny Zeller is known for her heartfelt stories of faith-filled happily ever afters and her passion to impact lives for Christ through fiction. Her books feature tender romance, steady doses of humor, and memorable characters that stay with you long after the last page.

While she has had a love for writing since childhood, Penny began her adult writing career penning articles for national and regional publications on a wide variety of topics. Today Penny is a multi-published author of over three dozen books and is also a fitness instructor, loves the outdoors, and is a flower gardening addict. In her spare time, she enjoys camping, hiking, kayaking, biking, birdwatching, reading, running, and playing volleyball.

Penny resides with her husband and two daughters in small-town America and loves to connect with her readers at her website at www.pennyzeller.com.

Hilltop Series

WYOMING SUNRISE

HOLLOW CREEK

LOVE LETTERS FROM ELLIS CREEK

PENNY
ZELLER
Love
FROM AFAR

PENNY
ZELLER
Love
UNFORESEEN

PENNY
ZELLER
Love
MOST CERTAIN

small town shenanigans

CONTEMPORARY ROMANCES

CHOKECHERRY HEIGHTS SERIES

Christian Romantic Suspense

Close Proximity

Mountain Justice